THE FURUBE SUTRA
(The "Shrugging Off")

Preparation Verse
Gather, tidy, and align your ways,
for they bring karma

Facing Self Verse
Cleanse any lies made this day,
scatter not one grain of life

Verse of One Resolved
To end this path in happiness,
seek peace within your mind

Three Levels of
THE EYE OF THE BEAST

1. Beast Sight
To link your mind to a creature and use its senses

2. Dual Sight
To see with your own eyes and those of a
linked animal

3. Sight-Control
To both see through and command a beast,
making it your spy or weapon

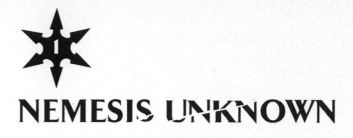

NEMESIS UNKNOWN

For glory or destruction. His master's saying tore through his mind again. Would a blade tear his flesh just as deeply before the night was over?

The sun would rise no matter what, but would Nanashi live to see it? He opened and closed his fists as the grim voice of fear began whispering. *It will be destruction, not glory,* it nagged him. *Tonight, you die.*

Taking a deep breath, he drove off the menacing thoughts and opened his eyes. How long had he been standing here in shadow, wrestling with this final wave of panic? Nanashi drew in the air as he studied the dark corridor ahead. By its cool scent, dawn was around two hours away. The moon had finally set. Darkness was his ally now. Nanashi crept to the end of the wood-paneled corridor and sank to one knee. He adjusted the sword on his back, turning his head left and right while he tried to steady his breathing. Stretching his neck, he listened. The chill night had silenced the last crickets outside. Now there was not a sound.

The great mansion was silent too, so he couldn't afford to make a single noise as he moved deeper into it. A cold breeze snatched sweat from his forehead and the hollows around his eyes. With it, a smell of stale bean soup from the kitchen found his nose. His nostrils flared, heart pounded.

Hearing only its thrumming in his chest, Nanashi shuffled noiselessly up to the twin sliding screens at the end of the corridor.

The heart of the mansion was a series of chambers, their thick walls made up of stained oak planks. Huge gnarled cedar beams crossed each chamber's ceiling, and the rooms were linked by narrow corridors and sliding screens inlaid with squares of oiled paper.

He hesitated, letting his heart slow, as he examined the runners of the screens before him. Beyond this barrier lay the last two rooms, and the objective he was desperate to reach. His stomach suddenly knotted. That objective would be guarded, perhaps by a team or just one, which would actually be worse. Any warrior posted alone would be their *best*.

Nanashi drew a small bamboo beaker from a hidden pocket in his black jacket. Easing the cork stopper from the tube, he hunched over one end of the floor slot that held the screens. Nanashi carefully poured water into its runner. As the liquid spread, he silently counted to five.

Tentatively he moved the nearest screen about a hand's width. It glided with a mere whisper. The water had stopped the screen grating noisily against the runners, just as he'd hoped. It was time. He would not think about the consequences of failure. For clarity, for strength, he would try not to think at all. He set his jaw and tightened the dark head-wrap that hid his smooth face. If he had to fight his way out, the guards would remember only his eyes. If he let them live.

Nanashi sighed. But of course he could not slay them. On this mission, the orders were rigid. Retrieve the documents. Take no life. No doubt Mantis had a hand in framing these rules. Him and his views! He'd get them all killed one day with that stuff. Nanashi pictured Mantis's gaunt face, his deep, ever-changing eyes: one moment hard with fierce resolve, the next glowing with pride bordering on tenderness. And, in almost every glance, a hint of sorrow. The boy momentarily hung his head. Mantis's beliefs made everything twice as hard! Nanashi wrestled his mind toward stillness and drew in the chilled pre-dawn air. Though veiled by cloth, his nostrils flared sharply.

Inside a nearby room, perhaps just two walls away, someone was sweating hard. The scent was of either an older man with a bad cold or a young, very fit man filled with tension. Both smelled the same to dogs, wolves, and foxes. And to Nanashi.

Training had not given him the heightened sense. It was what Groundspider called a "residue."

Nanashi had been trained in an ancient skill named *the eye of the beast*. At times, when he focused his mind on a nearby animal or bird, he could see through the creature's eyes, use its superior hearing, its powerful sense of smell. When that particular "sight-joining" was over, most of the beast-abilities quickly faded. Sometimes they lingered on in Nanashi after sight-joinings, serving him as the heightened sense of smell did now, but he knew that all such "residues" could vanish, without warning, at any time. If he relied too much on one during this mission then it abruptly faded—he stopped himself before that idea made his stomach twist into a new knot.

He gently opened both sliding doors. With the night-sight his special diet had given him, Nanashi scanned the unfurnished room ahead.

It was rectangular. A high, beamed ceiling. Plain side walls of dark-stained wood. Tatami floor...all reed matting. A single paper-covered sliding screen door broke the far wall. Still no sign of guards, but the scent of sweat was stronger now. It came from beyond that single door.

Nanashi carefully lifted one foot and made as if to enter the room. A detail just a few paces away caught his eye. He froze, stifling a gasp. Nanashi studied the floor of the room ahead. Strange little shadows. His heartbeat grew loud again. That was close. *Watch it,* he ordered himself, *there's no margin for error here. You almost walked into a trap!*

The floor was covered with neat, even rows of iron *tetsubishi*: sharp triple-spiked foot jacks, caltrops whose tips were probably flecked with poison. They were painted a straw color to make them blend in with the tatami. Nanashi slid the soft backpack from under the sword on his back and eased a bolt of rough black cloth from it.

Lining up the long axis of the roll carefully with

the distant screen door, he leaned into the room and flicked his wrists. The bolt quickly unwound in a straight line down the center of the tatami. Thinning as it turned, the spool crossed the floor with a faint hiss. Nanashi watched it, breath held. It ran out roughly three long strides short of the door. A complex potion smell, with hints of both persimmons and seaweed, escaped from the cloth. Though pungent, Nanashi was glad of its presence. Any spike penetrating the cloth shield would be coated with the dried potion, an antidote for *tetsubishi* poison. Most shadow clans soaked their *tetsubishi* in a formula that paralyzed, in order to capture a victim alive. It was no act of mercy. Only the living could be interrogated and forced to give up their secrets. Forced, it was said, with potions that unhinged the mind, and methods more dreadful still, which every spy deeply feared. Torture, by blade or fire.

Nanashi had made it this far, at least. This was the final door, if old Badger's archives were accurate and unspoiled. One could never be sure. The librarian's pet monkey had been known to deface his maps and charts in a variety of unseemly ways, and Badger, though he could speak and read in most known languages, was often unwilling to interpret his own charts for others. "You work it out, boy," he'd told

Nanashi a hundred times, "or your lazy brain will dry out like kelp flung on the rocks!"

Nanashi shook his head. *Thanks, Badger!* Well, last room or not, he couldn't leap quite that far, from cloth to door frame—not at that angle, anyway.

Moving on all fours, Nanashi padded slowly along the strip of cloth, spreading his weight evenly, testing each spot first with light, probing cat steps. As he put more weight on the thick, dense weave of the fabric, it caught and held the points of the surrounding *tetsubishi*. He paused, staring down nervously at his black highway. What if just one drug-coated tip burst through the cloth without being properly neutralized? Nanashi closed his eyes for only an instant, then forced himself forward.

He reached the end of the cloth and smoothly drew his sword from its scabbard on his back. Balancing on the edge of the tough weave, Nanashi stretched forward. Using the flat of his sword, he gently swept left, then right. With a soft tinkling, *tetsubishi* were flicked aside. He stood slowly, then took a wary step onto the new strip of floor he had cleared, sword held out before him, its tip hovering at throat height. Nanashi squinted at the path ahead, took three quick steps, and launched himself at the door.

He cleared the last *tetsubishi*, landing without sound in a crouch before the paper-covered screen. Nanashi glanced around, sheathed his sword, and once again carefully poured water into the floor slot to silence the screen runners. Then he rose to his feet, counting slowly as he redrew his blade. With its tip, he gently slid the door open. His nostrils flared again. The final chamber. So much would turn on what happened next. His heart beat out the rhythm of the words that had haunted him since sunset.

For glory or destruction. Now he would learn which would rule his fate.

This room, also a rectangle, was not completely empty like the last. Plain, dark wood walls, high ceilings with natural beams as before, but this final chamber also held a single piece of furniture. A squat Chinese-style writing desk stood at the far end under a shuttered, bolted window: a desk of stained cedar, a pressed gold hexagram on one side. Just as the plans had promised—the documents must be here. Nanashi's mouth went dry.

As always, he studied as much of the room as he could see before entering. No sign of any traps. The sweat smell was so strong here, there had to be a guard, coiled and ready to attack, tucked into one of the closest corners. But which one? And was there only one guard? Faint gnawing sounds came from behind the writing desk. Nanashi smiled as he smelled a rodent. His enhanced sense of smell, the residue of that last sight-joining he had experienced, was still working. How helpful! Some scribe had eaten here recently, and a mouse was seeing to the crumbs the maid had failed to notice. He sank to his knees and rested the sword across his thighs. Staring into the darkness, Nanashi aimed his mind at the source of the noises. His hands trembled momentarily. He took a deep breath, closing his eyes. The gnawing stopped. There was a soft scraping sound. Nanashi grimaced and pinched his nose: the odors in the room were suddenly overpowering.

The mouse crept out from under the desk, whiskered nose twitching fast, tiny twinkling eyes flicking up at the doorway.

As if now seeing through a thin, quivering layer of water, Nanashi saw, as the mouse saw, his waiting nemesis, crouching to one side of the doorway. This was no ordinary guard. The fellow wore a dark cloak and hood. Black unmarked armor showed beneath it. His head turned sharply as if he heard or sensed the mouse's movement. Nanashi's heart began pounding louder than ever. Inside the enemy's hood glittered a mesh veil. A straight sword hung on his back, assassin-style, but he also carried a hardwood bo staff. He was a big man too.

Nanashi reclaimed his sight from the rodent, forcing his own eyes to open. The usual fleeting moment of confusion jarred him, then he focused on the writing desk ahead. Just as his sharpening vision located the mouse, it looked up, then twisted and fled under the desk. An instant later he saw a blur of movement through the doorway, heard the swish of a whirling *bo*.

With blinding speed the strange guard sprung into view. He bounded forward, filling the doorway, swinging one end of his staff at Nanashi's head.

Nanashi barely dodged the blow. A wave of dis-placed air struck his eyes and he flinched as the staff hit the sliding door beside him with a loud *thwack*, snapping the wooden edging, tearing through paper squares.

Before Nanashi could respond, the attacker pulled his weapon clear then deftly drove it into a fearsome, humming spin. The *bo*'s tip became a blur, closing with Nanashi's temple!

Nanashi ducked under the whistling tip of the hardwood staff, then tumbled forward into a tight roll, brushing past the guard's leg and into the last room. Staying low, he turned and swung a cut at the guard's legs, but the *bo* ceased turning and dropped hard and fast to block the blade, which bit deeply into its wood. Wrenching his sword free, Nanashi rose, skipping backward to the writing desk, eyes wide at his enemy.

This man was both skilled and ferocious. That *bo* gave him too much added reach. It had to be neutralized! But how?

The attacker heaved a breath, then dashed across the room, spinning his staff again, moving quickly for one so large. Nanashi shuddered and braced for impact. His opponent bore down on him. The hardwood staff sang through the air, closing horizontally with Nanashi's neck. His heart thundering now like a drum, he parried upward with the flat of his sword, darted in closer, and aimed a powerful angular cut at the staff itself.

There was a dense splitting-tearing sound, then the *bo* clunked to the floor as two midget staffs. The large guard spun away in a circle as he drew the sword from his back with startling fluidity. Raising it in a two-handed grip, he started closing the distance between himself and his target at alarming speed, sword whistling as it arced in the air above him, tip poised to fly like lightning at Nanashi's forehead.

The smell of his own frightened sweat filled Nanashi's nostrils as he prepared for the response he knew best of all. A crafty set of moves, practiced a thousand times until they had become part of him. Now, his best hope of survival!

Turning one shoulder to the oncoming threat, Nanashi took up a low stance and faced an empty spot off to his opponent's side, daring the foe to take advantage of his awkward position. Only his eyes remained on course, locked straight ahead, judging the scant moments left before the attacker was close enough to strike.

Suddenly he was.

With desperate control, Nanashi rose fast, turning to face his opponent head-on and pouncing forward. The sudden turn and the change in both height and distance all combined to ruin the guard's timing. Before the man could slice downward, Nanashi's sword glided up into a fast, hard cut aimed at his raised forearms.

The blade bit home, folded steel grinding against concealed gauntlets. Focusing his balance and energy, Nanashi pushed with a muted grunt, forcing his opponent one step back. One step would be enough, if he could only make it count. He gulped in air, terrified of making the smallest error. Keeping pressure on the enemy's gauntlets until the last second, Nanashi whipped his blade back, then drove a powerful vertical cut down at the man's cloaked shoulder. A riskier target than his head, but the orders were to take no life.

The guard hoisted his sword into a strong block, but was a shade too slow to meet the incoming slice. There was a muffled clang, a sound of tearing cloth. Nanashi's blade glanced off the man's shoulder. The sword sliced open the guard's cloak, revealing the armor underneath, before flailing off to one side. Seizing his scant chance, the guard turned his own sword and lunged, blade leading the stretch of his long arms.

Suddenly the cold flat of its steel pressed at Nanashi's sweaty neck. He froze, lowering his sword. The guard had him!

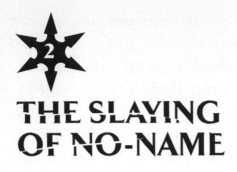

THE SLAYING OF NO-NAME

ext time you will die, in such a place, such
a moment."

The guard's voice was muffled, but his
baiting tone was clear enough. The armored giant
sheathed his weapon then peeled off his cloak and
plain black helmet. "Yes, it is me. Did you understand, Nanashi? You would have been slain. Right
here. Just now." Nanashi looked up at the broad face
of his daytime sparring partner, Groundspider.

From somewhere outside the mansion, a cock
crowed.

Nanashi untied his black head-wrap with one

hand. The cloth was soaked with sweat and, as it fell away, the cold night air stung his skin. He checked himself in the thin mirror of the flat of his blade, turning it slowly to sweep his long face. The flesh over both high cheekbones looked red. Beads of sweat surrounded his dark, cat-like eyes and dripped from his thin, straight nose and pointy chin. He licked salty droplets from thin lips, then flicked his thick tail of black hair with a regretful sigh.

Groundspider, alias the guard, eyed Nanashi with his ironic smile. His clean-shaven, aloof mouth twisted. "Cheer up! You're really fast now with that move, you know that?"

"Fast"—Nanashi slapped his own neck—"but dead. So what use is that speed?"

He sheathed his sword with a grunt.

"Look, it's not my place to explain." Groundspider shoved him affectionately. "But relax, kid!" He broke into a grin. "Always so serious! When are you going to become more like me? About to live or about to die, I still don't let anything worry me." Nanashi heard a familiar ring of mockery in Groundspider's voice. It was partly aimed at Nanashi, but partly at himself.

Despite his nervous anticipation, the boy cracked a reluctant smile in return. Though Groundspider's official role was to be Nanashi's sparring partner and to teach him the use of exotic, compact weapons such as throwing knives and smoke bombs, the big guy often assumed the role of his entertainer too. It came to him naturally. Hence, when required to go undercover during a mission, he excelled at playing extroverted roles out in the field, disguising himself as the cocky, gregarious silk merchant or the loud, buffoonish laborer. He was always the first to find the humor in things, to make light of disasters, even to poke fun at his own limitations.

They had much in common. Though older, Groundspider too had been abandoned as a baby on the steps of the Grey Light Order's orphanage in Edo. He'd also been raised and trained by the Order. But unlike Nanashi—or anyone else Nanashi knew—Groundspider was unusually tall and big-boned, like the offspring of a wrestler. With a bull neck and ox-strong shoulders, he had grown up displaying great physical power, but it had taken him most of his life to develop agility and stealth. Nanashi knew he would have found that discouraging, yet somehow Groundspider's long struggle to develop a light step amused the big man.

In fact, it inspired him to tell ludicrous stories about the consequences of his build: how much he weighed, how much he needed to eat. "When Heron found me, in a rice sack on the street before our gates," he had once boasted, "I was already so huge that she hurt her back lifting me, and needed the doctor's hot needles for a month." More recently, after surviving a tough rural mission in an isolated valley, Groundspider had bragged that while in hiding, his enormous appetite had forced him to consume—in one meal—three salamanders and an entire wild goose. Raw.

"But not the beak," he'd added solemnly, a wicked gleam in his eyes. Nanashi had called him a liar, and Groundspider had gripped his sword, face instantly fierce as if mortally insulted. Nanashi had flinched; then the big guy had laughed, clapping him on the back with the words "Still skinny and gullible!"

But today Groundspider was at least trying to be serious. He hastily composed himself as a lantern's light cut the dark of the next room. Nanashi peered back through the doorway. As the room grew brighter, he heard the sound of a swishing robe. Brother Eagle approached, a shine on his balding head, his long single plait of hair draped on his shoulder as usual. He carried a paper lantern on a pole in one hand, a broom in the other. Eagle stepped carefully, sweeping tetsubishi aside with the broom as he went.

In perfect time with each other, Ground-spider and Nanashi bowed. As they straightened up, Groundspider snuck Nanashi a glance that said, *Be brave.* Brother Eagle nodded to the pair with his typical secretive composure. He raised an eyebrow at Groundspider. "Report."

"The boy held back detectably," Ground-spider said, showing only his serious, respectful side. "Heeding our orders, no doubt, to take no life. His technique itself is now virtually flawless. It is definitely ready."

"But not him?" Eagle stroked his short, greying beard. "Say now, might he possibly have killed you, had no such orders fettered him? Had he been a touch bolder, his strike more confident?"

Groundspider looked thoughtful, then gave a single nod.

"Very well." Eagle grew solemn. "Then the true final—and first—test should take place in the field." He saw Nanashi break into a smile. "Mmm…" The long nasal sound told Nanashi that Eagle was thinking hard. "Your first real assignment. You may not be ready. But the world can wait no more. So it is time. You will shine, or you will fall. The fire must come from within. We've done all we can."

Nanashi dropped to one knee, lowering his head.

"I thank you, Great Teacher, but...have I not failed the test?"

"Enough. Rise." Eagle gestured impatiently. "Failed? No. In fact, you passed. We ordered restraint, tied your hands, as it were. So you concluded that this was a test of skill, didn't you? A skill challenge with a difficult handicap attached. Could you prove adept enough to steal the documents, defend and leave, with half your tricks forbidden by a no-killing order? You reasoned it thus, no?"

The boy stood up slowly and nodded, his eyes on the floor. "And I was not adept enough. I lacked the required skill."

"As everyone does." Groundspider grinned. "As a skill test, it's impossible. Nobody passes it. Any real mission so difficult would allow the use of equal force against the guards. Lethal force, just as they would use."

"I don't understand." Nanashi blinked, his eyes moving between his mentors.

"It is a test," Eagle said, nudging his arm with the broomstick, "of obedience, not of martial skill. How will this Nanashi react to missions he knows will end in bad wounds or worse? That's why it's always the last test before field trials. A test of character. You restrained yourself, as required. Your 'death' is the natural consequence of your obedience. You passed, my boy. The traditional reward, your graduation gift one might say, is something you have never owned. A real name." The two warrior monks exchanged knowing glances. Groundspider laughed behind his large, gloved hand.

"But I have a name." Nanashi shrugged. "Don't I?"

"Think back to that great, difficult day," Groundspider said, "the day you were moved from our orphanage beside the safe house to your life inside these walls. The day your training began. When we settled you in your little room, we renamed you then too, remember?"

Nanashi nodded slowly. "Brother Eagle said I could no longer be Go, for that was a child's name, and since I had been selected, I'd need a better one."

Eagle shook his head. "You were so excited to be chosen, yet sad to leave your friends behind. You knew our decision made you special, but also that the special are forbidden to revisit the ranks from which they came." He gave a faint sigh. "The special must walk alone."

Trying to recall the faces of the other children, Nanashi swallowed.

Eagle went on. "Hard it may be, but that separation is an old, trusted rule, part of our Veiled Way, and it works for the protection of all. Yet it cuts the heart, so it's no wonder you do not recall my words that day. I never said a better name. I spoke of a more appropriate one. Go, of course, is a name, but it also means number five. From the day Heron found your basket on our doorstep to the day you were selected for training, you were simply orphan number five. Once you were chosen, that name had to be tossed aside."

"And now," Groundspider added, "the time has come for a third and final change, where you take on the name you will keep until you die."

Eagle allowed himself an open chuckle. "We've never told you this, but *Nanashi* means 'no name.' From childhood to adolescence, throughout their training, each student we prepare, boy or girl, is called Nanashi. Our Order is small, our training intensive, so we develop only one high-quality candidate at a time, making their nameless name an easy secret to keep!"

Nanashi glanced at his teachers. "I wondered, you know, during certain errands outside the monastery…why some people looked curious when I gave my name. Now I understand."

"No doubt their manners made them hold their tongues, as we found with our previous candidates."

Eagle smiled. "If not, we would have had to tell you much earlier, and we do like to maintain our little traditions when we can. But it's true: everyone's a Nanashi until this very moment. Until their final test supervisor gives them a truly apt name, a title, really." He turned and gestured at Groundspider. "Traditionally, one names a successful pupil after a technique, strategy, or Old Country science they have mastered. Groundspider here, despite his bulk, excels at forest-floor concealment and ambush; hence he was named after the ancient Groundspider attack ploy. Now it is *he* who must shoulder the burden of naming *you*."

"Well, he almost had me with his signature sword move," Groundspider said. "The tempting angle, that sudden turn and the body's snappy rise, blade flying into a pinning cut across the forearms, then the push, before—"

"Ah, yes." Brother Eagle pointed at Nanashi. The older man's eyes lit up. "Your trademark sword defense...*tsukikage*. As I write the characters of that word, they also mean 'moonshadow.'"

Groundspider placed one gauntleted hand on the youth's shoulder. "So let it be. Nanashi has been slain. Moonshadow rises in his place." He stepped back, and, along with Brother Eagle, bowed to the new spy.

"Thank you." The boy returned their bows. "So it is, then...I am Moonshadow."

"Moonshadow of the Grey Light," Eagle spoke softly, "Mantis, with his zeal for Buddha, tried to teach you compassion as well as the art of dueling. Groundspider here, true follower of Hachiman, labored hard to school you in the war god's fury. Heed what each has taught you, along with all you've learned from Heron and Badger. But most of all, heed what I say to you now: young or old, it is our hearts that rule our fate." His face hardened. "For glory or destruction, as we say."

Moonshadow felt the maxim's words prickle his skin, but he nodded eagerly. "I am ready, Great Teacher."

"Indeed?" Brother Eagle looked thoughtful for a moment, then gave Groundspider a slight nod. "Leave us." Groundspider bowed and withdrew.

"Well, Moonshadow..." Eagle smiled as his student beamed at hearing the new name. "How you've developed! Your skills bring us all great pride."

At his teacher's praise, the boy felt his eyes grow hot. Eagle paused as if searching for the right words, then went on slowly.

"Soon you face the dangerous world as our outstretched arm, serving our master, the shogun, among his very enemies. So, as the head of our Order, I will need your reassurance about something."

"Anything, Master." Moonshadow began sinking to one knee.

Eagle motioned for him to stand tall. "Tell me this: when everything turns smoky, and your choices are veiled in dust, which voice will guide you? As I said, each of your teachers has influenced you according to his or her own view of the world. But whose voice will order your steps when chaos reigns?" Eagle watched him carefully. "Think on this, while I tell you a personal secret."

Moonshadow listened intently. Not only was he immediately curious — Brother Eagle never spoke about himself — but he was glad to be given time to think. Was this odd question a last, sneaky part of the final test? Perhaps, so he dared not get it wrong!

"I was not born knowing how to see through an animal's eyes," Eagle said. "I was born and raised samurai, with little awareness of the ancient shadow arts."

Moonshadow asked no questions, sensing the looming weight of Eagle's secret.

"As a young warrior I was chosen to serve as a *yojimbo*, a bodyguard, in an escort protecting the somewhat reckless — and unpopular — Lord Yabu as he traveled. He was a cruel man, who treated his peasants shockingly. He'd also made well-born enemies. High on a lonely stretch of mountain road, our rather gaudy procession was attacked by hired assassins from the Iga shadow clan. As was our duty, we fought hard, but Lord Yabu and his entire retinue perished that day…save for one youngster, taken prisoner by the Iga."

"You, Master." Moonshadow gaped at him.

Eagle nodded. "They held me in a forest stockade, hoping to learn all about Yabu's allies, but—despite their unkindest efforts—I told them nothing. In time, I even began to sense their admiration. Of course, regardless of Yabu's nature, I had failed to protect my liege lord, so I yearned to die. Then one night, the Iga themselves were attacked, by forces of the oldest shadow clan, the Fuma. In the chaos, I snatched a sword. My samurai upbringing told me to slay my Iga captors. Instead, I chose to save their lives. It placed them in debt to me. So unforeseen! But it was destiny."

The boy saw Eagle's stare drift far into the past. "Then they let you go?"

His teacher smiled sadly. "There was nowhere to go. I learned that during my captivity, my entire home clan had perished in battle, betrayed by Yabu's allies, the very men I'd endured torture to protect. My life as a samurai was over. So I lived on among the Iga, became one of them, and even learned their most ancient skill, which I've now passed to you. In time, a fateful mission brought me before the Abbot of the Grey Light Order. He was dying, and to my astonishment and disbelief, he bade the shogun have me take his place. Again, most unforeseen, but in hindsight, clearly meant to be."

Moonshadow looked up at him. "So it all worked out, both times, because no matter what befell you, you listened to yourself. Followed your own instincts."

"A fine answer." Eagle patted his shoulder. "Remember it when you get out there." He gestured with his shiny head to the world beyond their walls.

In the distance, a lone dog howled. Moonshadow listened as its mournful cry echoed, then faded. He smiled at Brother Eagle, hiding his thoughts.

Was that howl an evil omen? Did the old gods just tell me I am doomed?

THE TEACUP
AND THE WELL

Moonshadow woke an hour after sunset. He sat on his heels, legs folded beneath him on his bedroll, rubbing one eye and staring at the drab walls of his tiny room. His pre-dawn test had left him exhausted, though perhaps, he thought, it was really the sleepless nights leading up to it that had worn him out.

Three nights he had lain on his back from the midnight temple bell to dawn, staring at the ceiling, wondering what form his test would take, and if he could pass it. With it finally behind him now, he had obeyed Brother Eagle's last orders with great pleasure. Return to your room. Rest a full day and night. Then prepare your tools and clothes for your first real mission.

In the distance, through thin wooden walls and sliding paper screens, he heard Brother Eagle's voice once more, though the words were muffled. They drifted from the monastery's little kitchen, along with the sizzle of a cooking plate and the smell of spring onions lightly frying on it. Then he heard Heron speak. Her tone was unusually sharp. Moonshadow stood up and stretched, a rumble in his stomach telling him that the evening meal was being prepared just in time.

He glanced up at the narrow window high on one wall of his room. It was already dark outside, so he had missed the chance to intone his second *furube* for the day. Moonshadow sighed. The shrugging-off sutra was supposed to be uttered, its stillness entered into, each dawn and each sunset, as well as just before going into action.

Furube meant "shrugging off." *Shinobi* of both the Iga and Koga traditions had recited the sutra since ancient times, and most shadow clans had their own version of it. The *furube* served two important purposes. It refreshed the mind on a daily basis, helping the one reciting it to maintain calm, uncluttered thoughts, no matter what dangerous mission they might be on. The sutra's words also reminded a *shinobi* that despite having special powers, they were like any other human: their deeds produced consequences...*karma*. So the *furube* not only acted as a daily, ritual cleansing of the mind, it also realigned the conscience.

Moonshadow broke into a sly grin. He'd been warned never to skip it, lest that become a bad habit. But if he skipped it now, just this once, dispensed with reciting it late, who would know? Beating Groundspider and his huge appetite to the kitchen was surely more important. Groundspider could out-eat a sumo wrestler, maybe two.

Moonshadow slid open his door, slipped out into the darkened corridor, and followed the alluring smells. Now, ginger, pine nuts, and sliced radish were hitting the hot plate and the first at that long, low table would surely get the freshest, biggest serving. He was only two strides from the kitchen's sliding door when he heard Heron speak his name. Moonshadow froze, listening, hoping that she and Eagle were too engrossed in their conversation to hear—or sense—him loitering in the corridor.

"You've always been too protective of him," he heard Eagle say softly. "Maybe because it was you who found him that morning, thrown on our mercies."

Moonshadow sank into a crouch, controlling his breath lest their sharp ears pick it up. He turned his head to one side and parted his teeth to increase the range of his own hearing. Heron's reply was calm, but passion put an edge on her words.

"Come now, Eagle, have we not all grown fonder of him than perhaps we should? Besides, my concern is not some...motherly urge, it is professional."

"You heard Groundspider's report on Moonshadow's final test. Has he also grown confused? True, he treats the boy as a younger brother, but his opinion on such matters has always been sound. Moonshadow's raw talent is exceptional, and now, his skills are honed. Young or not, he'd vex any handful of good samurai and, in single combat, most *shinobi* for that matter. Don't forget how much extra work we've all put into him. You are wrong. He's our masterpiece, and he is ready."

"I don't doubt that his skills are ready," Heron said quietly. "But he is not. This may be the one flaw in our training process: he's tasted so little of life, of the world. Known so few people. His prowess is indeed remarkable, I agree, but the inexperienced make awful blunders. That is his weakness, and that may—"

"Cause him to fail?" Moonshadow heard Eagle scrape something from the cooking plate into a dish. "I say he will not fail. He will succeed and return to us alive. For two reasons. First, have you forgotten all the White Nun predicted when she pointed him out among the other orphans, while he was yet small and sickly?"

"No, of course not," Heron muttered. "And she's certainly been proved right about his rapport with animals. What's the other reason?"

Moonshadow edged closer to the door, fascinated. The White Nun! Groundspider had spoken of this unusual Buddhist seer, saying that she visited the Order once every few years, and was said to wield that Old Country science called Insight. Those skilled in Insight could discern a stranger's true nature, or glimpse things fate had in store for them. Was she the real reason he had been chosen?

Beyond the door, Eagle gave an irritable huff. "My second reason? I say he will not fail because he must not fail. So many dire missions await our agents now. This one, as you know, was never intended for him. It called for a face that our enemies wouldn't recognize, yes, but one more seasoned should be undertaking it. Moonshadow should tackle an easier task first time out. But as you also know, our original choice now lies badly wounded and, at last report, may not live to see next week. Our need is desperate, and if all the White Nun said about him proves true..."

"You are master of our Order and dear to my heart," Heron said slowly. "But please heed my warning. To send him on this mission, so inexperienced in all but the shadow crafts themselves, is to set a teacup on the edge of a well."

Eagle sniffed. "Then all we can do is hope that—" he stopped abruptly. Moonshadow heard the swish of robes and he turned and scuttled silently back to his room. As he slid his door shut, the kitchen door opened.

"Was that him?" Moonshadow heard Heron whisper. "How did we not hear him? Were we so caught up in our debate?"

"I told you he was good," Eagle mumbled. "How many could spy on us? You see? He is ready."

Moonshadow knelt on the floor of his room, pondering their words. Heron! She was always looking out for him, and though he felt close to most of his trainers, she was special. He had learned to trust her, show her his feelings in a way he could not with the others. Over the long course of his training, she had coached him in how to make smoke bombs and taught him combat with the short *naginata*, a pole weapon with a single curved blade. Heron had also schooled him in the use of disguises, poisons, and sleeping drugs.

Back in his tenth year, they had started to grow closer than teacher and student. He shut his eyes and began to relive that important hour. He had been a Nanashi then, that day Heron had told him who she really was...

The autumn sun was warm, leaves golden underfoot. Nanashi sat on a stone bench in the monastery's garden. Heron tutored him, testing his recognition of herbs and flowers whose essences were extracted to create shinobi *potions. Again and again he failed to identify the common flowers she found, picked, and brought back to the bench. Gradually, Heron's silken eyes grew hard and her deliberate, graceful walk stiffened. She fetched the final sample, a branch of a spindly herb. He didn't recognize it either. Heron sat down, hissed with irritation, and stared closely into his face.*

"Nanashi-Kun," she demanded, "why are you here, yet not here? Where is your mind today?"

"I had a dream," he confessed. "I keep thinking of it.

I saw two people. I think they were farmers." He looked up at her with burning eyes. "And they were my parents."

Heron's strong, dignified face softened at once. She ran her long fingers through his hair. "Poor child. I know something of loneliness too," she whispered. Heron locked her eyes on his.

"I think you already know that I was once a warlord's wife," she began. "High born, privileged. But few know how I came to serve the shogun in the Grey Light Order. I lived a grand but empty life in a mighty fortress. My husband, an honorable but distant man, lived only for training and glory in battle. My one companion, who slowly became my trusted friend, was an aging maid named Toki." Heron's face became taut. "One summer my husband led his army against our strongest foe. He fell and his men were scattered. Our castle was attacked and, during the siege, set ablaze. I took up my naginata, ready to fight to the death, but Toki stopped me, saying there was another choice. She told me the truth then: she was not who I thought she was, and I didn't really know her, but she loved me as one loves a daughter, and she could spirit us both away from the fire and the enemy."

"How?" Nanashi whispered. "Was Toki-San a sorceress?"

"No." Heron raised a long finger. "But she was no mere maid, either. Toki-San was a shadow clan agent.

My old, dear, only friend turned out to be a long-term infiltrator, planted in the castle during my youth by Clan Koga to spy for my husband's enemies. Yet Toki had not betrayed us to our foes. Having come to love me, she had chosen not to report to her masters for years. Toki believed the Koga thought her dead. It was not Toki, but my husband's rashness, his thirst for glory, that brought our fiefdom to ruin."

"But how did you escape?" Nanashi asked, eyes wide with wonder.

"Using smoke bombs, disguises, and the melee of the siege itself, Toki led me out," Heron said. "We fled to Miyajima, the island of the deer, where she taught me her secret arts so a pampered former Lady would not be helpless in the wide, hard world. We shared many peaceful years. Then I was alone, terribly alone."

Nanashi frowned. "But Miyajima is far to the west. How did you get here?"

Heron swallowed hard. "As Toki lay dying of old age, she begged me to go to Edo and seek a certain moody, brilliant scholar whom she'd long admired. I honored her last wishes. When I finally found him, the scholar had just been accepted into the shogun's service. You know him as Badger. On hearing my tale, he quickly realized that my training at Toki's hands gave me something to offer the Grey Light Order. Through his kind endorsement, my new life began. I took a new name, and I was never lonely again."

Sparrows flitted by in the afternoon sunlight as Nanashi wiped his cheeks. "I don't feel so lonely now either."

Smiling, Heron embraced him, cradled his head, and stroked his hair. "And you never will again."

A screen door slammed in the distance, snapping Moonshadow back to the present. He wiped moist eyes and sprang to his feet. Reaching that long, low table was now a matter of life and death.

Delicious, defenseless food lay waiting, and Groundspider was on his way!

Then Eagle's words rang in his mind. "…all the White Nun predicted when she pointed him out…"

His master's strange tone when saying it had alarmed him as much as the words themselves. Moonshadow hesitated, hand frozen on the sliding door of his room. What exactly had the White Nun predicted? Such a legendary seer wouldn't waste her insights on trivial things. Alongside hunger pangs, fear roiled in his belly.

The question persisted, like an itch in his mind. What *had* she foreseen about him?

NEW FACES ON PEACH MOUNTAIN

Silver Wolf paced up and down his empty audience chamber. With his hands clasped behind his back, the warlord hung his head as he muttered, scheming aloud.

His new team would be here any moment. A good variety of experts. But would they be able to work together? It was a blend of odd personalities. Would some end up fighting each other before they even met his enemies? The operation was turning out expensive too. One rather special hireling was going to cost him more than all the others put together....

Silver Wolf stopped and turned at the chamber's set of double sliding doors.

Light streamed in from the wide window at the opposite end of the long room, along with the sharp clicks of *bokken*, wooden practice swords, from the castle's inner courtyard below.

Near the window, Silver Wolf's battle armor hung on a T-shaped wooden stand. A low horizontal rack beside the armor held his two favorite swords.

Three paces left of the armor, a thick plank of white wood stood propped between the reed-mat floor and the windowsill.

He stared at his armor. Its leather war mask snarled above a breastplate edged with sculpted ribs. These days the tough, flexible suit was just a work of art for visitors to admire. Silver Wolf snorted bitterly.

In the final months of the long civil war, when the strongest lords had vied for mastery of Japan, he had proved a credit to his noble ancestors, showing himself fearless in battle. Leading his men under the Tokugawa banner, Silver Wolf had helped crush the aspiring shogun's enemies, handing him power over all the land. And what had been his reward? It had hardly matched the promise he had received, the one that had induced him to fight so daringly.

The would-be shogun had pledged that once the land was united under his rule, Silver Wolf would lead an invasion of the Korean Peninsula. As the shogun's favorite captain, he would expand the empire, carving his clan's name into the great stones of foreign castles, where he'd forever be remembered as a conqueror. What a lie! Instead, he'd been given a small chest of gold. With it had come an announcement that had turned his veins to fire. That infernal edict.

For soon after tasting victory, the new shogun had embraced what he called a fresh vision. A dream of a new, peaceful Japan, a realm of art and flourishing culture...like a garden of flowers, the edict had read. A land of supposed balance that would neither invade its neighbors nor let newcomers, like those strange barbarians from the far end of the world, gain influence. Silver Wolf and his boldest allies had been ordered to forget the past. Outrageous! Forget their pride? Forget what this very armor stood for?

Their new leader's change of heart had cut them more deeply than any foe's blade. They had put him in power and once there, he had insulted their warrior blood.

The emperor, of course, would never intervene to set things right. Though held to be a living god, he was in fact a tiger without teeth, a figurehead only, who would never challenge anyone with an army at their back.

No, it was up to Silver Wolf. His eyes refocused on his armor. A work of art! Not for much longer. Not if all went well.

He started pacing again. He didn't feel like a traitor, like a turncoat plotting rebellion. No. He was a rescuer! It was their so-called greatest military leader who had betrayed every nobleman, every samurai in the country. What deserving shogun wanted an end to the birthright of battle?

Serenity. Peace! Such things were not for warriors! Silver Wolf gritted his teeth in contempt. The shogun's very title meant "chief general who subdues barbarians." Yet it was barbarians who would help Silver Wolf subdue this foolish shogun. It was his duty to remove the traitor. To replace him. To restore the pride of the nation.

He pictured his new foreign allies. Their round faces, eerie blue eyes, strange clothes. So few of his countrymen had encountered these men of the far West, who called themselves Europeans. He smiled grimly. So few would want to, seeing as they didn't bathe daily as all Japanese did. Worse still, they ate their meals, not with chopsticks like the civilized, but with a knife—a weapon—and their bare hands.

Those barbarian traders, who cared only about money and opportunity, had already played their greedy part. But before he could make use of what they had sold him to topple the shogun, an obstacle had to be overcome. The shogun was no mere fellow warlord, to be easily crushed with a surprise border attack or well-timed treachery. His secret service men were no amateurs either; they were possibly the best warrior-wizards alive.

Silver Wolf's rugged face tightened, stretching the long scar on his left cheek. The Grey Light Order. For generations, the secret defenders of each shogun's life and office. Only a handful of lords had even heard of them. It was whispered that their name itself was a warning that they belonged to no normal world, phantoms existing between darkness and daylight. Shadows of the twilight and the grey of early dawn, their skills and ways were veiled in myth and superstition. But their agents were real enough, and they would certainly come after his new weapon, even before it was built. He nodded with relief. At least they were not the only spies in the land, and most others, the warriors of the shadow clans, would serve anyone who could afford their hefty fees.

His gaze moved to his sword rack. Once his sword smith turned those plans into a reality, no amount of armor would save the shogun or his men. After all, slow loading, single-shot firearms were everywhere these days. They were dangerous enough. But no one had even heard of a gun that could fire multiple lead balls, one after the other, and with improved accuracy.

He imagined the shogun's armored cavalry and lines of spearmen charging his own ranks boldly, expecting his gunners to fall back and reload, as theirs had to, after each volley. Their mouths would fall open beneath their leather war masks when his men simply went on firing, round after round, his new, unique firepower mowing down man and horse like a sickle passing through weeds.

If his project could only reach completion, he, Lord of Momoyama Castle, would be invincible. Silver Wolf tapped his cheek with one finger. He was ready to intercept their agents, destroy them, and all without getting his own hands dirty. Art and culture! He shook his head.

"We're a race of warriors. The destiny of warriors is war," Silver Wolf grumbled. "The rule of the strong, not artists and thinkers!"

In the courtyard below his keep, the shouts and clicks of samurai practicing swordplay abruptly stopped. The voice of his chief guard broke the pause, ushering someone toward the tower. They were here.

It was time to gauge if, so far, his money had been well spent.

Silver Wolf strode to a small padded platform near his swords and suit of armor. Set at one end of the bland, rectangular room, the platform rose as a symbol of his superior status. It was the only elevated, cushioned part of the long chamber's tatami mat floor. He sank to his knees on it and rocked back on his heels, tidying his lush robes, straightening his pointy cap. As he waited, Silver Wolf's gaze drifted around the wood-paneled walls then up to the beams crossing the ceiling.

The double doors slid open. The chief guard, a stocky samurai with a wrinkled, scarred forehead, stood between them. He bowed low to his seated master then gestured over his shoulder. "Your…guests, Lord."

Silver Wolf motioned for the arrivals to be sent in. The chief guard stepped back, waving five men into the audience chamber.

The warlord looked the group over with a slow nod. Two of them he knew well: burly samurai, each wearing two swords, hand-picked from his own household guard troop. One of these locals was very tall, the other short but exceptionally muscular.

The other three visitors were quite something else again.

"Since you new faces don't know each other,"

Silver Wolf said slowly, "let us begin with introductions from all three of you."

Silver Wolf pointed to the scruffiest of the new men.

The youngest of the trio was a wily-looking fellow with a thick, messy beard and drooping moustache. His long, untied hair was tangled and he wore a bright, patterned jacket that was popular among town gamblers. His neck and forearms were covered in detailed red and green tattoos of carps and dragons.

"I am Jiro, Lord," the man said, bowing quickly. His beady eyes darted from side to side. "Throwing knife specialist and slayer. No job too small, no target too unusual."

The pair of household samurai glanced at each other. It was clear from their expressions that they weren't happy working with a gangster. The warlord smiled. He understood their feelings and truly, Jiro was the worst kind of scum, but he was useful scum. His obsession with money meant he would act without question and, if anything went wrong, he could quickly be blamed for the whole plot and sacrificed to the shogun's head-chopper. It wouldn't be right to waste a loyal samurai in such a way.

"My men don't seem to like you." Silver Wolf grinned. "It's nothing personal. It's just that they are proud samurai, and you, after all, are a lowly criminal. They don't realize yet what a useful fellow you can be...if what I've heard is true." He gestured at the white wood plank leaning against the windowsill. "Show me. A straight line. Top to bottom."

Without hesitation, Jiro the gangster fished in his jacket. He took a step forward and his right arm flashed three times in a whip-cracking motion. Fast swishes cut the air as black blurs flew from his outstretched fingers and three sharp *thwack*s made everyone's eyes dart to the plank.

Silver Wolf smiled. Three black *shuriken*, star-shaped throwing knives, stuck from the white wood. They formed a perfect vertical line. Jiro grinned, wagging his head from side to side proudly. As he turned to the men beside him, he raised one eyebrow.

"Impressive." His nearest companion nodded. Older than Jiro, this newcomer was balding, wiry, and clean-shaven. He had pitiless eyes and wore a plain black robe. "But are you as good with a target that fires back?" the wiry man asked, giving a little sneer. He turned to the warlord, gripping the sword on his hip as he bowed elegantly.

"Great Lord Silver Wolf," he announced, "I am Akira, a professional of two schools. I gather information. I silence enemies."

Again the two household samurai exchanged glances, but this time their faces spoke of recognition and respect.

"An aging professional," Jiro mumbled.

"What's that you say?" Akira gave the gangster a menacing snake-like smile then glanced at their employer. "I'd be happy to demonstrate that second skill, right now, if my Lord wishes, on this gambling peacock…."

"Your swordplay comes highly recommended by my allies." Silver Wolf held up a hand. "So, in your case, no demonstration is necessary. But I will require a show of patience, and proof of your ability to work in a team. From all of you!"

Akira bowed sharply. "Of course, Lord." His eyes flicked sideways to the only hireling in the room who had not yet introduced himself. "But I don't know all who grace my Lord's new team."

The tall, well-built stranger he spoke of turned and slowly looked Akira over before bowing to Silver Wolf. All eyes locked on the mysterious man. He was the only man present who was openly wearing the dark night garb of a spy or assassin.

Silver Wolf studied his most expensive hireling. A straight sword hung from the man's back and his face was covered by an unusual hood. It was fashioned from one long strip of indigo blue cloth, wound many times around his head, and secured with two small knots, one just above each temple. Though the knots looked like small, bristling ears, nothing about the stranger struck anyone as funny. His unblinking black eyes, smooth movements, and lurking aura of physical power made him an unnerving figure.

"This, gentlemen," Silver Wolf said with pride, "is The Deathless."

"I thought The Deathless was a myth." Akira frowned. "A story to frighten children." He gave the hooded agent a quick, polite bow. "No offense."

"A folktale, that's right," Jiro blurted. "Nobody could live up to that reputation! I've heard it said The Deathless is immune to sword cuts! Impossible!"

A deep, confident voice came from inside the cloth hood. "Not just sword cuts, little man." The fixed stare of The Deathless swept over Jiro before the killer bowed low to Silver Wolf. "My Lord, may I still these foolish tongues with a demonstration?"

"Why not?" Silver Wolf gave a low chuckle, trying to disguise the fact that even he was unsettled by this man. "But don't kill anyone... this operation is expensive enough already!"

"My Lord." The Deathless strode, head held high, to the center of the audience chamber. He smoothly unsheathed his sword then pointed its tip at Jiro.

"Gangster!" He grunted. "Come, kill me! Show our Lord how you will take down his foes!" He cocked his hooded head to one side. "You *have* actually killed someone before, haven't you?"

With an angry snort, Jiro quickly drew three more *shuriken* from his jacket. He hurled the first at The Deathless's head. The tall assassin bent his knees and bobbed under its flight path. The whirling black star streaked into the wood paneling directly behind him, embedding itself with a loud *thwack*.

"Concentrate, dice-roller!" The Deathless sniggered. "You just wasted your best chance!"

Jiro cursed and threw the next *shuriken* at his target's chest, but The Deathless raised his blade at the last possible second and blocked it. A spark flew from the sword. The black throwing star buzzed skyward to wedge in a ceiling beam.

The two household samurai were openmouthed with awe. The shorter one nudged his partner.

"They say that under that hood," he whispered, "he has the head of an otter, but with huge fangs."

Akira glanced up at the *shuriken* in the beam and nodded slowly to himself.

"I'll show you!" Jiro growled. He flung the third *shuriken*, this time at his enemy's stomach, then drew a small dagger from his jacket and rushed The Deathless.

Silver Wolf blinked as the gambler charged. His third *shuriken* had simply vanished. What magic was this?

The tall assassin let his sword droop as Jiro whistled past, slashing the dagger hard into his chest.

Silver Wolf leaned forward, breath held.

The Deathless made no move. Jiro slowed, regained his balance, and spun around, raising the dagger and pointing back at The Deathless with it. "Looks like the Lord's money will be wasted. On you!"

A low, superior chuckle came from beneath the knotted hood. Silver Wolf studied The Deathless carefully from head to foot, then he too began to laugh.

Jiro's eyes widened as The Deathless held up the third *shuriken*. He had snatched it from the air itself with his free hand. The tall assassin sheathed his sword on his back, tossed the *shuriken* at Jiro's feet, then, with both hands, stretched the cloth of his jacket tightly over his torso.

"What?" Jiro's head snapped forward. His lips twisted in amazement.

A distinct cut now marred The Deathless's jacket. But beneath it and the slashed white undershirt, his skin could be clearly seen.

There was no blood. There was no cut.

Jiro inspected his dagger. It was dry. He shook his

head, stumbling over his words. "How? How did—I know I cut you! For sure! I felt it! Nobody can—"

"It is rumored," Akira put in solemnly, "that The Deathless was trained by the shadow master, Koga Danjo himself!"

"Koga Danjo is said to be three hundred years old," the short samurai whispered.

"Take note," Silver Wolf warned the group, "our invulnerable friend here charges by the kill, not by the day, so I will be holding him in reserve until something worthy of his talent crops up." He nodded to Akira and Jiro. "Meanwhile, you pair, supported by my best two swordsmen here, should be able to deal with any lesser visitors."

"Does my Lord expect more than one intruder, then?" Akira folded his arms. Silver Wolf nodded grimly, patting the floor at his side. "Momoyama Castle…Peach Mountain Castle." He sighed, his stare gliding to the ceiling. "It is a strong fortress, yes, but built to withstand a different kind of attack from the one now coming. Have no doubt, our land is full of spies and counterspies these days. And there will be other hopeful takers out there, keen to snatch my new prize."

"Other warlords may vie for the plans?" Akira rubbed his smooth chin.

"Yes. Though sitting atop this keep, secure in my archive room, ringed with loyal steel, the agents of other ambitious men will try for them." He waved his hand along the line of mercenaries. "But with my guards and you gentlemen ready to intercept them, what should we fear?"

"Exactly." Jiro stuck out his chest. "We won't fail."

"Good." Silver Wolf smiled, then caught the eye of The Deathless. "If you do…"

The Deathless slowly looked Jiro up and down, then turned back to his master and bowed. The gangster forced a nervous grin.

"Dismissed!" Silver Wolf grunted.

Unseen servants pulled the sliding doors open. As one, the hirelings bowed and turned to go. The two household samurai darted forward and collected the *shuriken*, using their short swords to pry them from the ceiling beam and wooden wall paneling.

The warlord of Momoyama waited until his audience chamber had been cleared, then hung his head and whispered, "Who could possibly stop us?"

WARNINGS ON THE GREAT ROAD

Moonshadow grinned as he trudged along the road. The fine spring weather itself was enough to make anyone smile, but a heady feeling of freedom doubled his joy. There was so much to see, smell, and hear, all of it totally new. Over the course of his life, he had left the Grey Light Order's base, the monastery in Edo, many times. At first, he had just run shopping errands, designed to help him practice basic good manners and to teach him to handle money responsibly.

Then he'd been made to play games like "errands in disguise," delivering or collecting coded messages, and later, there had been simple spying missions. Along the way he had seen different kinds of people. But never a variety like this, for never had he traveled so far west along this highway, the Tokaido. Around him now were folk from town and country alike, walking, running, or limping. Men, women, and children of all classes. And more females of around his age than he had ever seen before. He shook his head as a short, mop-headed girl struggled by, hefting a large backpack. No wonder armies were made up of men! He sighed, shaking his head. With the exception of Heron, it was clear that girls and women just weren't cut out to be warriors. Moonshadow watched the short girl drop her pack and stop to rest, taking big gulps of air. How did ladies even survive with so little strength?

Not long out of Edo, he suddenly found a distant set of large eyes meeting his idle gaze. They belonged to a peasant girl of about his age. She was walking alone with a pack on her back and a staff in one hand. He noticed her smooth skin, tiny nose, and full lips, but what kept him watching was her obvious strength. She was tall and lean and took long strides with a straight back as if the pack's weight was nothing to her. Perhaps he had been wrong and there were a few girls as strong as boys? Without warning she smiled at him. Moonshadow stopped walking, looked away, and hoped she hadn't noticed him staring. He pretended to study a tall tree beside the road, hoping that by now, she had moved on.

After a while he turned warily and scanned the road ahead. The girl was far away, moving at quite a pace into the distance, obviously trying to catch up with a small group of farmers about to disappear over the rise.

She reached them, and his discomfort eased. Then they were all gone.

Moonshadow chided himself to stop wasting time and to get moving. He glanced back in the direction of Edo, and a pang of emptiness went through him. He suddenly realized that he missed the daily sight of Eagle, Heron, the grumpy Badger, Groundspider, and even Mantis, despite his hard training and endless platitudes. The Grey Light Order was the closest thing he had to a family. And as exciting and new as everything was, out here in the world, part of him already longed for…home. The world is a lonely place, he thought, for those who are alone.

But an interesting place, too, filled with curious new faces. That girl, the cute, strong-looking one, there was something about her. She'd worn the clothing of a peasant, but for one of that lowly class her face had seemed too…confident? No, that wasn't the right word.

He shook his head. What was wrong with him? What did a strange peasant girl matter when such an important task awaited? Moonshadow hurried on. A long road and its dangers still lay ahead.

Many called the busy Tokaido "The Great Road." It ran from the eastern capital of Edo, the shogun's home, twisting west and southwest through mountains, along the sea, and over many rivers to finally reach Kyoto, where the emperor lived.

Moonshadow repeatedly checked the lush forest on both sides of the road as he walked. It was well known that many parts of the highway were unsafe, plagued with bandits, cut-purses, and tricksters. These menaces used all kinds of force, lies, or clever schemes to relieve travelers of their money and weapons, and sometimes even their clothes. For peasants, the nobility, and even for the shogun's officials, travel meant taking risks. Unexpected danger could prove as close as that next bend in the road or shadowy glade.

An old man with one arm stepped into Moonshadow's path. He smelled of plum incense and waved a paper charm above his head shouting, "For sale! Luckiest luck ever! Only three copper coins!"

Moonshadow quickly skirted him, head down, pacing twice as fast until the luck salesman gave up.

He had noticed that almost all traffic on the Tokaido moved on foot. Apart from the warrior class, few owned horses and much of the road was too thin, steep, or rough for carts. The wealthy and noble were carried in litters or palanquins, fancy boxes suspended between poles that were shouldered by two or four strong bearers. Around each settlement, inns, food, and gift shops lined the highway. Moonshadow watched in fascination at one town as a rich merchant was carried in a gold-painted litter up to the porch of a tavern. Leading his litter bearers, the merchant's samurai bodyguard shoved aside a straggly outcast who sat begging for food scraps near the porch.

The Hakone Barrier awaited him ahead, and Moonshadow hoped he would pass it without incident. The highway went through over fifty towns and villages between Edo and Kyoto. Where it crossed from one warlord's fiefdom into another, checkpoints were set up. They were guarded by spearmen and samurai. Only those with identification papers could pass. Any caught trying to sneak over or who presented forged papers were executed on the spot.

Moonshadow knew his travel documents were real, approved by the shogun himself, but he had been warned that arrogant, overbearing samurai had made mistakes at checkpoints before. Cocky barrier guards had been known to take an instant disliking to some travelers. Legitimate messengers and even holy men had been mistakenly executed.

Before leaving Edo, Moonshadow had memorized the monastery's chart of the Tokaido. There was, at least, no danger of becoming lost. He could see the route clearly when he closed his eyes. Well past the forested mountains of Hakone that now rose in his path, he'd turn off the highway to head south, then east, to the town of Fushimi. The lair of Silver Wolf, the lord of Peach Mountain Castle.

He recalled how Badger had described this warlord. A ferocious, battle-tested veteran, outwardly loyal to the shogun, yet—according to Grey Light Order intelligence—plotting dire rebellion. A ruthless, cunning man, Badger had said.

Moonshadow passed through a village where a new wave of travelers flooded onto the road of packed earth and fine gravel around him. Each person's clothing identified their profession or place in society. Moonshadow studied the unfamiliar uniforms discreetly as he drifted among them, gathering fresh disguise ideas.

There were peasant farmers with baskets or frames on their backs. In these they carried vegetables, sacks of soybeans, and drums of rice and grains. He saw teams of porters, burly, sweaty men in matching jackets who were paid to carry other people's luggage. Clerks in "company" robes, each with an abacus tucked under his arm. Some were only boys, working as record keepers and store men for wealthy merchants.

Moonshadow followed the rising, winding road into the forest near Hakone. The trees became taller, the scrub denser. The road itself grew shadier. Massive, swaying groves of giant bamboo appeared on both sides of the highway. Close, convenient hiding places for bandits!

Suddenly the flavor of the travelers around him changed again. He noticed fewer townsfolk on the road now. There were many more farmers, all moving in groups for safety. Moonshadow spotted a few unemployed samurai too, those known as ronin or wave men, warriors without a master. Swords for hire!

He felt his tension grow as more of them appeared. Unpredictable wanderers, they were everywhere these days. Moonshadow watched a tall, proud swordsman strut past, chin held high, worn kimono barely holding together. The fate of such men was a sad one. Vast armies had been officially disbanded or scattered by defeat when the civil war ended, leaving thousands of warriors adrift and idle, without Lord or purpose.

No wonder so many had lapsed into lives of drinking, illegal dueling, or banditry. Brother Eagle had wisely called them a great, unsightly wrinkle in the new age of peace, a problem for which their master the shogun must find an honorable solution.

The highway was also dotted with priests, monks, and most importantly for Moonshadow, pilgrims of all ages. Their presence would help make him invisible on the road, for today, he was just one of them. Most pilgrims, he knew, would be heading for the famous and popular shrine at Ise, where prayers and wishes were said to come true.

To any barrier guards inspecting him, Moonshadow was a typical boy pilgrim off to Ise. He wore a wide, conical straw sun hat, brightly painted with spiritual slogans. A drab brown weatherproof cloak, tied round his neck, extended to his knees. A long, wadded indigo jacket peeped between its lapels. Wide strips of dark cloth were wound about his legs. Rough strawcord sandals were tied on his feet. On his back hung a pale reed-matting bedroll, so that like most pilgrims, he could sleep in the grounds of shrines or temples as he traveled. Unlike most pilgrims though, his bedroll hid a sword and a kit full of unusual tools.

Below his holy traveling cloak, which was made from layers of oil-soaked paper, hung two cloth prayer-scroll bags. They held his *shuriken*. Under the crown of his sun hat lurked a small percussion-triggered smoke bomb.

He carried more silver and copper coins than a regular pilgrim too. Money to rent lodgings, to buy food and new weapons, or to bribe informers. The coins were buried deep in his belly-binding cloth, which, apart from serving as a money belt, had two other purposes — to hold in the wearer's core warmth during cold nights on the road and, as the writing on it said, to bring him good fortune.

For a moment he caught himself daydreaming, lost in the perfumes of unfamiliar roadside flowers, in the strange accents of passersby. Then a squirrel caught his eye, scampering between oak trees at the side of the road. Moonshadow stopped and grinned at the flitting smudge of grey fur.

His eyes lit up. These new sights and sounds made him feel bold; the world looked full of wonder and possibility. It was time to try an experiment.

It had been Brother Eagle who had trained him to "capture the eye of the beast," to enter an animal's mind and harness its eyes and other senses for a brief time. Eagle had told him that beyond the basic beast sight, there were two higher stages of the ancient science. The second level was dual sight, where one could see through a creature but still use one's own eyes at the same time.

And then there was the third and final level: sight-control. It was the ultimate stage of the craft and could only be employed on complex animals. As the name implied, it went further than the use of an animal's senses. For during sight control, one could make a beast obey one's wishes, turning it into a deftly controlled weapon. The swooping hawk, the prowling bear.

He stared down at the squirrel, reaching out to it with his mind. It stopped its skittish ambling and blinked back at him, nose twitching. He would use it to try for the second level: seeing through its eyes and his own. Moonshadow had managed this a few times before, though only during supervised practice sessions with Eagle, and only ever in tiny, unstable bursts that fell apart without warning.

Moonshadow hesitated. He was out in the open, and this was perhaps a slightly reckless thing to do, but who would know? What could really go wrong? He closed his eyes and his hands trembled. Immediately, the squirrel's view of the road's edge appeared, distorted through what looked like a quivering layer of water. Then the squirrel-vision shifted to the road ahead. The animal's gaze locked onto the last teahouse before the climb to the great ridge, and

Moonshadow smelled tofu cooking in soy sauce. Linking with an animal sometimes caused a heightening of his human senses. Today that side effect was strong. Moonshadow's nose twitched and his stomach tingled. He smiled. Good, so far it was all working well. Now to try for level two.

The sound of straw sandals crunching grit underfoot came from somewhere off to his left. Moonshadow's instincts warned him to break the link with the squirrel and check the source of this sound with his own eyes. He severed his tie to the animal and started forward for the teahouse, scanning left and right with peripheral vision. His mind felt a little cloudy after the joining, and Moonshadow realized that in such a public place, surrounded by so many strangers, his daring experiment had been a bad idea.

A stocky ronin samurai was loping towards him. Did this mean trouble?

Pretending to watch the road ahead, Moonshadow studied the one approaching. The stranger wore a single sword, belted and tied as if he knew how to use it. He was not very tall, but his steps were long, so he was flexible, and there was energy in each stride he took. His hands dangled at his sides, but his fingers were still, as if controlled. The samurai appeared relaxed, yet his eyes were locked on

Moonshadow and he moved as if with purpose. A concealed purpose. There were no scars on his face, so either he didn't fight much, or when he did, he won. Was he an enemy agent?

If so, it hadn't taken Grey Light's foes long to make a move!

Wait. Moonshadow set his jaw. What if the fellow was actually harmless? This was a public place and he must not draw attention to himself unless there was no choice.

The samurai quickened his pace toward Moonshadow, then raised one hand and pointed at him. Moonshadow felt his stomach muscles tighten, his body readying itself for attack. At any moment the samurai would be close enough for a sword strike.

Should he snatch out a *shuriken* and be ready? Moonshadow knew he could not ignore the man for much longer. He would either have to run or stop and find out what the warrior wanted. Or wanted to do.

Duelists and assassins used the element of surprise. Was this the stranger's plan? Get close and launch a sudden fast draw? Then it would be too late to react, wisely or not.

Brother Eagle's most frequent advice came back to him now.

Never react too fast. Think before you pounce.

Moonshadow stopped walking, carefully taking in the potential threat with sideways glances. The stranger's left hand rose from his side, brushing the scabbard of his sword. Moonshadow felt an urge to bound to the right and draw a *shuriken*. Eagle's voice rang in his mind, stopping him. Moonshadow's eyes flicked to the samurai. If caution was the wrong response, this man would speed-draw any second now and cut him...or kill him. The stranger's left hand scratched his belly hard through his jacket.

"Oi!" he grunted. "You! Kid!"

Moonshadow held his breath. He was now within reach of the man's sword. He wanted to spring clear, but instead turned to face the samurai and bowed, hiding his wariness of the stranger's next move.

"Yes, sir?" Moonshadow forced a smile. "May I help you?"

"Yes! Hire me!" The warrior gestured uphill with one hand, gripping his scabbard with the other. "Otherwise, they'll kill you! They're waiting just ahead, you know!"

Moonshadow gasped and looked quickly in all directions. Who was this samurai? Who were these enemies he spoke of?

How had his cover been ruined so quickly?

6

A HARD FIRST TEST

Was the man an agent or not? And was he friend or foe? Moonshadow stuck to more of Eagle's training: when uncertain, never admit anything and never assume anything.

"Who would want to kill me?" Moonshadow asked with wide eyes, a tremor in his voice. To be convincing as an unarmed boy pilgrim, he had to seem vulnerable. "I am but a humble traveler yearning only to pray for my sick mother at Ise."

The samurai pointed uphill. "To get to Ise, first you must get through Hakone. Just over the top of this ridge is the barrier. Past that, the thickest, darkest bit of the forest. That's where pilgrims, young ones especially, go missing all the time. Bandits take them!" He scowled, elbowing Moonshadow. "But not the ones who hire themselves a *yojimbo*!"

The man had used the formal word for bodyguard. Moonshadow had last heard it spoken during Brother Eagle's account of his ill-fated service to Lord Yabu. So that was it. The ronin was an out-of-work samurai bodyguard. His tale about bandits was probably a lie, but this fellow was no servant of Grey Light's enemies. He was all about money.

"Well, I don't know about other pilgrims," Moonshadow said, "but I can't afford a bodyguard. Very sorry. I'll have to take my chances." He bowed and turned to walk on.

"Wait!" The man scuttled into his path. "Just for you, I'll make an exception. Forget cash if you're hard up! Your bedroll would cover my fees nicely." His face darkened. "I insist you accept my generosity!" One hand moved to his sword. He took a half-step forward.

Moonshadow sighed. Here indeed was a neat trick: this slimy clown's game was to rob people with a kind of polite bullying, using the threat of imaginary robbers lurking over the next hill. A hard first test out in the world! How to get rid of this man without drawing unwanted attention? Moonshadow's eyes darted across the road to the teahouse. Above the little wooden hut flew a banner, reading: REFRESHMENTS! LAST CHANCE BEFORE BIG CLIMB.

"I can see you're right; I do need protection," Moonshadow said carefully. "And the truth is, I was given some coppers, begging at a shrine a few towns back. But that hill…" He groaned at the steep path rising ahead.

The samurai followed his gaze and then frowned. "What? So it's steep! It's also the only way you'll get to Ise."

"Yes, of course." Moonshadow pointed to the teahouse. "Let's get a chilled tea though, before we tackle the hard part. I'll use those coppers to buy us both one."

"Now you're talking!" The stranger paused and wagged a finger in his face. "But it doesn't change our deal about the bedroll."

"No, no, of course not." Moonshadow led him to some empty stools on the tiny porch outside the teahouse. As he walked, he carefully fished in his belly-binding for some copper coins, then for a tiny object wedged next to them: a bamboo phial sealed with a cork plug. He smiled secretively.

While studying under Heron's guidance, Moon-shadow had always found the science of potions, particularly flower and herb identification, somewhat less than inspiring. But today he felt grateful for Heron's knowledge of herbology. The beautiful, dignified woman was surely the land's greatest expert in poisons of every kind, and she had taught him well.

Moonshadow urged the samurai to sit and relax while he bought their tea. The serving lady filled two clay cups, then stooped to clean her wooden ladle in a stone basin. Before turning back to face his unwanted companion, Moonshadow deftly flicked three drops of black liquid into one teacup and returned the phial to its hiding place.

"There, sir." He put the drugged cold tea down before the samurai, then cheerily held up his own cup. "To our success. And...to the ruin of all thieves!"

The stranger grunted in agreement, draining his cup in two fast gulps. Moonshadow smiled. This one's gluttony would work against him. He sat down, listening to the birdsong of the forest, watching the passersby, while he counted silently.

When he had reached sixty, he glanced at his would-be bodyguard. The man's eyes were already half-closed and his head was lolling forward. Moon-shadow sprang to his feet. "I must be going now, sir. I can see you're not yet rested, so, farewell!" He bounded from the porch and started pacing away uphill. His sharp ears told him that the samurai had struggled to his feet and was swaying on the spot, leaning on creaking furniture.

"Oi!" the man called, his speech slurred. "You can't go. You need me. My sword is...I am...I can't be...defeated!" He gave a sharp belch.

Moonshadow glanced back over his shoulder. The samurai raised one hand, pointing, then his head sagged onto his chest. The hand flailed, dropped. He swayed a full circle, then tumbled headlong from the porch to land facedown in the road. A small dust cloud rose around him.

The serving lady hurried from her shop and leaned over him, tilting her head to one side. Her face creased with surprise. The samurai was already snoring loudly. She returned to the porch, snatched up his teacup, and peered warily into it.

Moonshadow shook his head and quickened his pace uphill. He looked back one last time with a grim smile. "You won't be drinking here again."

THE BARRIER

Within an hour, Moonshadow crossed the ridge and the road descended, snaking into a shady gully where it met the Hakone Barrier. There a wall of sharpened bamboo stakes ran right across the gully. Behind the wall was a little guardhouse. A heavily protected single gate loomed in the wall's center. To one side of the narrow opening, a warning flag read:

PRODUCE PAPERS, TURN BACK, OR BE ARRESTED.

Opposite it, a long banner proudly declared:

SUSPECTED SPIES BEHEADED SO FAR THIS MONTH: ELEVEN

Eleven executions in two weeks! They couldn't all have been real spies. Moonshadow forced himself to stay calm, though his thoughts quickly sped up. In recent times, the shogun had encouraged the regional warlords to staff these checkpoints with their own samurai. It saved the shogun money and helped keep his own loyal warriors around him in Edo, but it also created problems. Some local samurai were overzealous at their job or just plain bullies. This particular crew was made up of Silver Wolf's men, and they seemed eager to be as ruthless and feared as their master.

Moonshadow eyed the warriors ahead as he drew closer to the barrier. From the way they lurched and strutted, all show and no real balance, his dueling instructor, Mantis, could have fought them all and won. He almost smiled. Of course, Mantis's advice right now would be to avoid trouble: adopt a soft tone and show patience, even when such manners were not deserved.

Moonshadow glanced at the road behind him. No sign of his unwanted bodyguard, who would still be sleeping off his special tea for some time to come. Moonshadow vowed to be more careful of strangers from now on, to protect his mission from all delays and distractions. His orders, after all, were straightforward and urgent. Enter Silver Wolf's lair. Find and steal the plans he had just purchased, plans for a new type of weapon, and so neutralize their threat to the shogun. He paced up to the barrier, one hand dipping in his jacket for his papers.

"Halt!" A gruff voice roared. Moonshadow heard the *snick* of a sword leaving its scabbard and he froze, closing his eyes the way a frightened pilgrim boy should. A blade whistled in the air to his right, and he felt its tip pass close to his neck. He sensed the guard on the other end of the sword, another warrior stepping up behind him, and a third swordsman to his left, half-drawing a blade slowly and noisily.

"We tell you when and how to reach for your papers! Understand, boy?" the samurai behind him demanded.

"Yes, sir." Moonshadow nodded quickly. He opened one eye.

The guard to his right slowly withdrew his sword and sheathed it. "Let's see them, now!" he grunted. "Left hand only." Moonshadow followed his orders, slowly pulling his identification papers from his jacket. Each barrier guard carefully studied the document, reading the description of the young pilgrim, then inspecting him to ensure that he matched it.

"Hmm. I think it's him. All appears in order,"

one guard said casually. He glared at Moonshadow. "But I hate religious beggars. Let's kill him anyway." The others nodded.

Moonshadow thought quickly as he stared back at the man's stony face. These guards were mad dogs! If they made a move, he would have no choice but to take down the closest ones, then run. Maybe they would spare him if he pleaded? He tried to look defenseless. "But…sirs, please. I didn't do anything!"

"Oh yeah." The stone-faced guard suddenly grinned. "That's right, you didn't!" He looked around, sniggering. "What are the rules again? Oh, that's it. We should only kill the guilty ones! I guess we'll have to let him live after all." He slapped his thigh and gave a high-pitched giggle.

The other guards laughed too, one clapping Moonshadow on the back. "Did you see his face? Why are pilgrims all so gullible?" He snorted, then guffawed. His laugh had an annoying nasal quality that made Moonshadow want to duel with him.

"It's 'cause he's just a kid." The third samurai yawned, obviously tired of their game now. He thrust the papers into Moonshadow's hand and waved him through the gate. "Go on, holy boy, get out of here! May the gods help you make it down to the lake. Bandits have been bad this month."

Moonshadow strode away downhill, muttering angrily. He hated being called gullible, perhaps because it was one of Groundspider's favorite taunts. Nice sense of humor, those guards! If it wasn't for the wisdom of Eagle and Mantis, he might have overreacted twice on this, his first day on the road, throwing away the whole mission. Why did everyone keep on about bandits though? Like the ronin he had been forced to drug, surely those barrier guards had been lying, just teasing him again.

Then his eyes flicked ahead, taking in the look of the highway. Overhead, the tree canopies were starting to meet, forming a long natural arch. The forest below was the darkest stretch yet. A white stone marker beside the road caught his eye. He stopped as he reached it, kneeling down to read the inscription below its cap of thick green moss.

It was a list of names, apparently several members of the same family. Down one side of the little monument, a line of text said they had been slain.

By bandits. In this forest.

So it really was a dangerous area! Outlaw gangs had been widespread since the chaos of the civil war years. The shogun's men now hunted them down, but in mountain country like this, finding every group was virtually impossible. Some bandits were clever, accomplished ex-warriors with local knowledge on their side.

Moonshadow felt his heart grow heavy for these victims. Since their survivors could afford a marker, the family were most likely rising merchants or minor nobles. Perhaps they had journeyed to establish a new outlet for a business or to attend a relative's wedding, only to lose their lives tragically.

He sighed. These people would have had bodyguards, but for it to end this way, bodyguards were clearly not enough. Had brave hired ronin died fighting to protect them? Or had their hirelings run in cowardice, leaving them to the bandits? Moonshadow swallowed, then offered a quick prayer for the slain.

He stood up, staring at the marker. The inscription was just weeks old. Moonshadow began to walk downhill, then stopped and looked up into the thick canopy. He turned his head left and right, mouth open, listening.

Every bird in the surrounding forest had abruptly stopped singing.

BRIGANDS OF THE FOREST

A hundred paces downhill at a sharp switch-back in the road, a large group of farmers huddled together.

Moonshadow studied them. There were around two dozen men and women, in roughly equal numbers. Perhaps from the same village or at least the same region, they ranged from an old, stooped couple to a handful of youths.

Pressing into each other, back to back and shoulder to shoulder, the farmers peered into the tops of the trees just as Moonshadow had. The forest's ominous silence continued. An older woman, in a series of frightened whispers, urged the group to stay still and quiet.

Moonshadow tightened the chin sash holding his sun hat in place. He hurried to catch up to the huddle of fellow travelers, but as he trotted under the forest's darkest archways yet, he questioned himself.

What exactly did he plan to do when he reached these people? He was supposed to make it to Fushimi unnoticed, undetected by any of the shogun's enemies. Now he found himself considering what spies called Overt Combat—using one's skills publicly—and this was strictly forbidden unless he had no choice.

So what use could he be to these poor farmers? He wasn't obliged to protect them. In fact, if they were attacked, he wasn't allowed to protect them.

He was supposed to take the easy option: escape. What happened to these defenseless people was simply not his problem. In fact, they would be helping him by tying up the brigands' attention while he stole away. During the chaos that would surround the bandits robbing their victims or carrying them off as slaves, he could vanish through the forest and go about his mission. Why was he even considering helping out? Had Mantis and his endless maxims about Buddha's compassion scrambled his mind?

He said it aloud, struggling to convince himself. "Not my problem."

As he closed with the group, Moonshadow glanced up and saw a familiar face.

It was her.

The peasant girl smiled with recognition. He blinked in pleasant surprise then stared at her. She wore that look again. What was it? A quiet strength, he decided. Why did it seem familiar?

Moonshadow was ten paces from the girl when the first horseman burst between the trees. The farmers went into a tight, gasping crush. The ground rumbled. Branches snapped, twigs crackled and flicked into the air as three more riders charged from their hiding places. Moonshadow turned a smooth circle, looking the attackers over. Two were archers, the other two spearmen. All four brigands wore armor, but not one of them had a matching set. Most likely they had pilfered these mixed fragments from the dead of some great battlefield. Each rider was a patchwork of randomly colored plates as they galloped in circles around the screaming, praying farmers.

While the others squeezed together the girl alone stood tall, gripping her staff like a sword, eyeing the riders with cool contempt. Moonshadow shook his head, motioning for her to join the protection of the group. She ignored him. Without a thought he started making for her. At the same time, one of the horsemen slowed, stopped circling, and trotted his mount straight at the girl.

Moonshadow hesitated, mind racing. His mission...guard its secrecy...not his problem...

Her eyes met his and she smiled again. Moonshadow steeled himself. He was unsure how or why, but some part of him had already reached a decision: a quiet escape was now out of the question. But he also had to conceal the nature of his skills as much as possible. There'd be no going for his sword.

The mounted spearman closed quickly on the girl. Moonshadow put his head down, grunted, then ran hard and fast for the brigand. There, he'd committed himself to the fray. Now what? Without a sword, just how was Moonshadow going to stop him?

TRICKS OF COMBAT

The idea came to him just in time. As he dashed up to the bandit's horse, Moonshadow pulled a *shuriken* from the pouch inside his jacket, hiding it in his hand so that only a few dark, sharp spikes peeped between his fingers. He twisted his body, right arm lashing out in a horizontal arc. A split second later, when the rider noticed him and raised his spear, Moonshadow cartwheeled out of range.

Ignoring the girl now and glaring at Moonshadow instead, the brigand pulled hard on his reins, turning to chase his new target. His mount took another stride or two, then the wide leather strap holding its saddle in place came apart, a neat cut-line suddenly opening across the strap's entire width. The saddle lurched, slid to the right, then tipped forward, breaking away from the horse. Dropping the spear, the brigand toppled from his mount, turning in the air with a frightened squeak. He landed on his back beside the scrambling huddle of farmers. The strongest men quickly expanded their circle to surround him.

Moonshadow was already running for his next target when the bandit sat up, dazed, only to find himself ringed by the very people he had been about to harm. The farming men glanced at one another, nodded, then pounced on the fallen spearman. He went for his sword, but two men trapped his arm before he could draw it. Behind the melee, a mounted bandit archer hoisted his bow. He took aim at one of the farmers pinning the downed brigand's sword arm.

Unnoticed by all but the girl, Moonshadow sprang into view beside the archer. His arm briefly becoming a blur, he hacked in the air like a cat cuffing a dangling thread, then dropped to the ground, landing in a low crouch. With a loud *fff-twang*, the rider's longbow bucked on the end of his arm. Its wooden curve straightened out, dipping sharply as its arrow launched and string snapped at the same time.

The mounted archer howled with pain and began snatching for the arrow that had just pierced his foot. Moonshadow scrambled out of sight behind the bandit's horse. With gritted teeth and an angry sob, the archer slid from his saddle. He hit the ground hard then curled up, muttering painfully, trying to loosen the arrow that pinned his sandal to his foot.

Moonshadow stood up. The two remaining brigands were riding straight for him, one from each side. The first brandished a bow, the second a spear.

He waved frantically to the girl, catching her eye. "Get them ready to run," he shouted. "When I signal you, go, and don't look back!"

"Who are you?" she called, her eyes wide. "What are you?"

"A..."—his mouth hung open for a second—"a... warrior monk!"

Moonshadow slapped the rump of the wounded bandit's horse and it started turning in panicked circles. He darted, low to the ground, toward the looming mounted spearman.

The rider changed the grip on his spear and thrust at Moonshadow impulsively.

Moonshadow evaded the stab and grabbed the

spear's shaft in his free hand, leaning back as he secured his hold. With a twist and a grunt, he tugged it from the man's grip. Spinning around, Moonshadow tossed the spear, point-up, to one of the feistier farmers.

The disarmed brigand roared at Moonshadow and fumbled for the sword hanging in a sheath below his saddle. Moonshadow sprang up to the horse, deftly cut the spearman's saddle strap with the *shuriken* in his hand, ducked into a fast roll under the animal, and came up running on the other side. As he streaked off, the saddle strap gave way and the bandit, with sword half drawn, crashed from the horse in a fast, uncontrolled somersault.

Now only one of the robbers, an archer, remained mounted. He turned sharply to see Moonshadow accelerating at him. Cursing, he quickly raised his bow and nocked an arrow.

Tucking the *shuriken* into his jacket as he ran, Moonshadow charged in a zigzag for the final enemy. The archer let fly. His shaft whizzed into a blur that passed within two fists of Moonshadow's neck.

Leading with his hip and shoulder, Moonshadow deliberately crashed into the side of the archer's horse, startling the animal. As it shied sideways, whinnying, he grabbed the rider's stirrup and foot with both hands, twisted, then pulled hard. The archer gave an agonized cry and let himself slide from the horse to stop his hip from dislocating.

Springing clear as the archer fell, Moonshadow turned a circle, hands raised defensively like knives, eyes darting about. He checked each opponent before giving a single, crisp nod. It was done: he had unhorsed them all, and without resorting to his sword.

"Go!" he yelled to the girl. She nodded, beaming at him, then threw him her staff. Moonshadow caught it and held it up in salute. The girl urged her companions to run.

As the farmers rushed off downhill, matching their pace to the limits of the oldest among them, Moonshadow took the staff between his hands and set himself to block the road should any of the brigands remount. He glanced over his shoulder at the fleeing group.

He saw what he had hoped to see. There she was, at the edge of the throng, shepherding the others, looking back every few seconds, watching as long as she could. Watching for more danger, or just watching him?

Moonshadow smiled and nodded, then turned back to guard the brigands. He sighed. Any moment now she, along with the farmers, would vanish from sight around the bend, off to the safety of the lake district at the bottom of the great Hakone ridge.

Should these robbers try for a comeback, at least now he was freer to act. While it mattered what farmers might witness and go on to describe at a festival or in some crowded tavern, it was of no concern what a bandit saw. No one would believe anything they said, so Moonshadow could now do whatever was called for. Were they still dangerous? He cautiously inspected his foes. In the forest canopy above, the first birds resumed singing.

The original brigand Moonshadow unhorsed had been knocked out by some farmer's solid punch and although heavily bruised, he just looked asleep. His comrade with the arrow in his foot was still curled in a ball, whimpering as he gingerly tried to pull the shaft free. The third bandit Moonshadow brought down had cut his arm with his half-drawn sword while falling. Having lost a lot of blood quickly, he was pale and weak. He struggled to tie a tourniquet around his arm with a trembling hand and his teeth. The fourth unsaddled robber was trying to get to his feet using his undrawn sword as a crutch. Judging by his twitchy movements and constant wincing, the man's leg had barely stayed in its hip socket. He would be useless for combat for weeks.

A sudden feeling of guilt gripped Moonshadow. Back in the monastery, he had passed his final test on the grounds of obedience. Had his intervention with these bandits not been just the opposite: a reckless act of defiance, in which he'd risked his entire mission for a bunch of farmers? His mouth tightened. Or was it actually worse than that? Hadn't he really taken this huge gamble over a girl?

If Brother Eagle were standing here now, there'd no doubt be sharp rebukes for bending the No Overt Combat rule. He frowned thoughtfully. Mantis, however, might actually praise him for showing kindness to strangers, chivalry in defending the weak and helpless. Groundspider, of course, would just revel in the thrill of the fight! Badger—as always—would agree with Eagle, while no doubt ponderously quoting some ancient Chinese sage, and Heron, well, she could go either way. It was all so confusing! He looked the bandits over again, thought of the girl, and then filled his chest with air. No. His inner voice had bid him to act. Like Eagle himself, who had spared his Iga interrogators so long ago, Moonshadow had made a fast decision based on his own instincts. Whatever he had just done, he didn't regret it. He would live or die with its karma, its reward or its punishment.

Moonshadow checked downhill again. No sight

or sound of the farmers now, nor hints of dust rising from the highway. He grinned with satisfaction. They had made good their escape. Which meant she had.

He looked back to the stricken bandits, feeling a little cheated. Moonshadow thought about frightening them with a smoke bomb vanishing illusion. Such a feat would leave the rogues convinced that a *tengu*, a long-nosed, tree-dwelling mountain devil, had attacked them disguised as a pilgrim boy.

Moonshadow grumbled to himself. Why waste the smoke bomb? Even if the trick worked splendidly, so what if he scared them? That too would be a waste. None of them could run anywhere. He sighed. He would end up having to just stand around and listen to them scream. Watch them thrash about on the ground or stumble hopelessly as they tried to flee the *tengu* smoke.

"Some other time," he mumbled. Moonshadow turned and scurried downhill.

Don't foolishly think it will be this easy, a cold instinct warned him. *Your real mission is a hundred times more dangerous. And if you hit the ground, no one will spare you.*

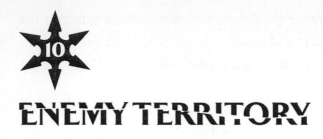

ENEMY TERRITORY

The drizzle had finally stopped, though the sky remained overcast. Heavy grey clouds, along with the towers and roofs of Momoyama Castle, loomed over Fushimi.

Moonshadow squeezed through the inn's small, crowded eatery, the box containing his new writing kit under his arm. Before closing the sliding door between the noisy diners' lounge and the corridor to his tiny room, he scanned the seated, feasting lunch patrons. Three married couples, two traveling hawkers, an old lady pilgrim, a middle-aged samurai, and five townsmen whose jackets said they worked for the local sake brewery. Near the door, a family with three noisy toddlers.

His instincts told him they were all what they appeared to be.

After defending the farmers, Moonshadow's remaining days on the road had passed without incident, perhaps mostly because heavy spring rains had settled in, forcing everyone on the highway to seek shelter or move along faster.

Just before dawn that morning he had crept into Fushimi, inspecting the town from the vantage point of the highest roof he could find. He had scanned its layout until he was confident that the depths of his mind would retain the details of what he had seen. Then, after stealing a new disguise from a back courtyard's drying pole, he had checked into this, the cheapest-looking inn.

Moonshadow was now dressed as a long-distance mail boy, complete with a small wooden post box–backpack and a faded running jacket marked MESSENGER in large script. He frowned as he paced down the corridor, smoothing wrinkles from his jacket. Though some believed it was bad luck to ever kill a messenger, his enemies, who were most likely both close and numerous, probably didn't. But he would not concern himself with them yet.

It was time to prepare, to draw up a sound operations chart, not worry about who might be on his tail. Let them show themselves first, as foes with less training always did. In the meantime, he had to ensure the silver coins he had just spent weren't wasted. Moonshadow closed his room's sliding door, sank to the reed matting, and opened his writing kit.

He took out and unfolded a large sheet of handmade paper. Then a brush, a stick of black ink, a small, grooved ink stone, and a clay water beaker. After pouring some water into the stone's groove and dissolving part of the ink stick into it, he dipped his brush and started drawing a map of Fushimi.

Moonshadow had learned a technique named passive recall. The trick was to stare at a diagram or scene—in this case, the layout of a town—until the information sank deep into the mind. Heron had called the knowledge "the fly," his will "the spider," his deepest memory "the web." To later recall the information and capture it, one chose to remember, set a brush in motion, then simply let the conscious mind wander. Guided meditation honed the skill.

At first, this notion of daydreaming to produce an accurate chart had sounded ridiculous. But he'd learned that passive recall enabled more accurate map and plan drawing than everyday methods.

"Only we *shinobi*, we spies, use this way," Heron had told him, her gentle eyes watching his eager face as he handed her a copy of a diagram she had made him memorize. "It's another example of our greatest strength: our power comes from knowledge that ordinary men have lost—shards of Old Country sciences, from an age when people were wiser and closer to the land."

Moonshadow's brush moved slowly, in time with his breathing. He glanced up.

The cramped, rented room was not a lonely place. At least two mosquitoes circled overhead at all times, and his first glance at the floor had warned him of the presence of other, equally tenacious invaders. Hence his second purchase this morning—a carved bamboo tube full of white flea powder—was as crucial to his survival here as his sword. Moonshadow cursed his accommodation but then, despite himself, smiled. This horrid little room reminded him of the map-drying booth behind the Grey Light Order's library. Smelly, musty, and confining as that other tiny chamber was, remembering it always made him grin.

One particular incident there repeatedly came back to him. It was a day on which Brother Badger, the Order's archivist and tutor on military history and battlefield theory, had—yet again—lost his beloved monkey Saru-San. Moonshadow shook his head. Though Badger, in his life before the Order, had been a scholar, his pet's name was not very clever, since Saru-San meant Mister Monkey. Not a very nice monkey, either.

Moonshadow, or Nanashi as he had been back then, was ordered to check the map-drying room and other nooks and crannies for Saru and several missing brushes. The creature was mindlessly destructive, but it also stole things for futile hoarding—food, tools, even children's toys from nearby homes. Saru would hide them all pointlessly, then fly into a rage when he couldn't locate them.

Interestingly, Moonshadow recalled, Badger would also misplace things, then become irritable while searching for them. In fact, Groundspider had once whispered that Saru and Badger resembled each other, both in their personalities and looks. He observed that both were balding, with slightly pointy, randomly scratched heads and very yellow teeth.

"The same dull eyes..." Groundspider had teased. "They could be half-brothers."

That fateful day, Nanashi had entered the drying room, dodging freshly painted hanging maps that swayed from the ceiling rafters. Holding up a paper lantern, he had searched the dark corners for Saru. The animal's sudden screech overhead startled Nanashi. He raised his lamp only to find the largest, most detailed map torn and ruinously streaked, with Saru smudged from snout to tail in its wet, recognizable colors. It was one of Nanashi's tasks to repair damaged maps or redraw them from scratch.

He cursed the beast. With twinkling eyes, Saru waved a dripping brush at him.

"You're a demon!" Nanashi had growled, stamping one foot at the monkey. "Come down now, I'm dragging you straight to Brother Badger." He hoisted the lamp under Saru. "Monster! Drop that brush! At least you've already done your worst!"

The monkey had stared at him, cocking its head to one side as if pondering his words. Then it raised its eyebrows, turned its back, and lifted its tail. Nanashi sensed the hairy little fiend's plan too late. Cursing, Nanashi had turned to flee the unusual attack from the rafters. In fast, foul seconds he would never forget, his lantern was doused by the most terrible of all monkey weapons.

"I'll kill you! I mean it this time!" Nanashi had fumed, backing out the door, as Saru mocked him with triumphant chatter from above.

He had bumped into Badger, who'd started

yelling, "What's happened? This mess! What a stench! Oh no, my maps!"

Moonshadow grinned broadly. Only after all this time could he find that day funny.

He pictured Badger's stare that Groundspider called "a dull look." Moonshadow remembered the conversation that had changed his attitude toward the grumpiest of his tutors. It happened after the drying-room debacle, in the heart of winter, when the monastery grounds gleamed with fresh knee-deep snow....

Nanashi sat opposite Badger on the library floor, endur-ing a long, dry lecture on the history of shinobi *on the battlefield. Nanashi yawned openly. Narrowing his eyes, Badger suddenly shuffled closer. Nanashi cringed, half-expecting to be slapped for rudeness. Instead Badger spoke softly, a trace of amusement in his eyes.*

"You think me a drab trainer compared to the others, do you not?" Badger raised one hand. "Don't answer; spare me a roughshod denial. Why, you wonder, is this crusty old scholar here? He's no warrior, therefore unwor-thy of respect." Badger watched his victim squirm. "Well, let me impart a different history, then. Hear what a

man must sometimes do, faced with... too much respect."
Nanashi saw his earnest expression and listened as never
before.

"I was not always called Badger, of course," the archivist said. "That is my Order name, given ironically no doubt, because the animal denotes patience. I was once a traveling teacher, and an author of battle manuals. My name then was... Hosokawa." Nanashi gasped. "Yes, that's right." Badger smiled. "I don't just draw maps and translate. Half the published books you've studied here... I wrote them."

Nanashi glanced around the library, struck with awe. The Hosokawa! His works were required reading throughout the warrior class.

"When I was Hosokawa the famous writer," Badger continued, "I chanced one summer to be lecturing in Tanabe Castle... the very week it came under siege. An unusual affair, that siege, for few armies use cannons—so hard to transport in our mountainous land—yet a row of fine, imported cannons was lined up facing Tanabe's walls. But when the artillery captain learned that I was inside and might come to harm, he delayed firing, telling his men he loved my books, and would avoid my accidental hurt at all costs. He was in a hard position: his general, who was on the way, had ordered a relentless bombardment.

"So he fired all his cannons many times, but not one was ever loaded with a cannonball. On arriving, the general demanded to know why the castle walls still stood. His captain politely claimed he'd forgotten how to load the cannons. Apparently, on later hearing the real reason and my name, the general exclaimed, 'Hosokawa? I love his work! You acted wisely, Captain. Hosokawa must not die; I want his autograph!'"

Badger laughed, then his face clouded with sadness. "He bade his men take the castle without using cannons. The hard way—just ladders and a battering ram. His army captured Tanabe all right, but a third of them died doing it. No harm came to me, and the general got his autograph. When I learned all this, long after the siege, the burden of it split my heart. I withdrew from public life, never publishing again. Instead, I answered the shogun's call"—his voice became a whisper—"to slip into the grey light, to be one of its phantoms, to live only as a secret guardian of peace."

From that moment on, Nanashi had found respect for Badger, worked hard in his classes, and tolerated both his abrupt manner and his stinking, pesky pet.

Back in the present, Moonshadow blinked and stared down at the paper, brush drooping in his hand.

Passive recall had proven itself again. While dreaming of the past, he had completed his map of Fushimi without apparent thought. As Heron once told him, distracting the mind with memories helped unleash that sunken knowledge. Now the map had to be checked with his conscious mind. He studied its wet lines, starting with the image of the great castle and moving clockwise around the page as he compared the map with his dawn memories. Every detail had to be right.

His planning—his life—depended on it.

BATTLEFIELD·FUSHIMI

The town of Fushimi was set among low rolling hills, beyond which sharp mountains rimmed the horizon. The original folds of the handmade paper had left creases through Moonshadow's map, dividing it into four equal quarters.

In the top left quarter, his brushstrokes showed Momoyama Castle, surrounded by a wide moat and linked to the town, downhill from it, by a single, heavily guarded bridge.

The top right quarter of the map depicted the tangle of drab buildings, massive round wooden vats, and bamboo pipes that made up the sake brewery.

Along with the castle to its left, it occupied the highest ground in the area, overlooking the town. A long, high cargo cable was suspended between the brewery and the castle. Lord Silver Wolf, renowned for loving sake, had obviously set this up so he could have barrels of his favorite drink cabled directly into his fortress.

On the bottom right quarter of the page, the map showed the main road leading into town near a small shrine and a *torii* gate, a simple, four-beamed wooden archway marking the entrance to a holy place.

In the final, bottom left quarter, his brushstrokes conveyed the grid-like streets of the town itself, sprawling away over a fold between the low hills.

Moonshadow put down the brush, watching the ink change hue as it dried. The map looked correct, so the procedure now was to check it again, add any last details that came to him, then sit still, staring at it, until he could see it perfectly whenever he closed his eyes. If interrupted, or if he sensed another study session was required, he would hide the map in the ceiling of his room in the interim. Keeping it on his person at any time would be too dangerous. If injured, caught, and searched, it would be bad enough that his concealed weapons would reveal him as a spy. The discovery of the map would do something far worse:

it would help his enemies confirm his mission, making life even harder for any agent replacing him. Once he felt complete confidence in his knowledge of the map, he would burn the page and scatter the ashes, since ashes too could be read by a trained eye.

Only one detail would be omitted from the map, in case it was discovered: his escape route once the warlord's unique and dangerous secret plans were obtained. An unmarked and little-known trail, carefully described to him only as he left the monastery, wound east through the countryside near Fushimi to a gorge where the Order's agents would rendezvous with him.

Precisely where that trail began and the day and time of this meeting were crucial secrets he could never commit to paper or speech. He had been told these things at the last possible moment for a good reason. A *shinobi* might face sudden capture at any time, and the less each one knew, the safer the others would remain. Moonshadow sat cross-legged on the floor, eyes moving over his map again and again.

Abruptly, his warning senses bristled. He turned his head, listening. The babble of voices, the click of chopsticks from the dining area as a distant door opened. Footsteps. No unusual or alarming sounds, and now he could smell the man approaching down the corridor, a man who ate too many *mochi*, the highly addictive rice sweets. Moonshadow knew who owned that syrupy smell in these parts. The innkeeper! After making certain the ink was dry, he quickly folded the map into an intricate flat knot. Next time he checked, he would know if anyone had opened it.

"Thanks, Heron." He smiled fondly. "Another useful trick you taught me." As he stood, tucking the knotted map into his belt, Moonshadow remembered Heron once handing him a tiny, perfect paper reindeer. It was a reward. Young Nanashi had maintained neat grooming over the course of an entire week!

Heron would be proud of him now, he thought bashfully. Since meeting that bold girl on the road, Moonshadow had found himself washing his face more carefully each morning. He took greater care in tidying and tying his hair, too.

He snatched a deep breath, then vaulted from the matting up into a corner of the room, wedging himself like a great insect where two walls and the ceiling met. With one palm jammed against the nearest rafter, his legs spread wide and the soles of his feet pressed to the converging walls, Moonshadow yanked the map from under his belt. He slid it carefully into a cobweb-lined gap between the top of the rafter and a ceiling plank. Lazy knocks made the sliding door tremble. He dropped quietly to the mat, straightening up just as the door started to open.

"Aw! You are here." The innkeeper's flat forehead was beaded with sweet-smelling sweat. He was a plump, friendly fellow whose eyes and movements told Moonshadow he had taken a genuine and kindly interest in him. The innkeeper thumbed over one shoulder.

"Young sir... a man awaits you, outside on the street."

"Me?" Moonshadow frowned. "How does he even know of me?"

"Who can say?" The innkeeper's voice fell to a whisper. His eyes narrowed. "He's been questioning all the young men roundabouts. Be careful. I don't recognize him, but I think he may be a policeman. It's... it's the probing stare!"

The innkeeper gave a warning scowl and turned away. Moonshadow swallowed. A policeman? Just what he needed!

UNWANTED ADMIRER

Moonshadow peered out through the inn's front door. On the porch a small row of flags hung from a ceiling drawstring that was taken down each night. The flags were painted with bright characters that read: OUR ROOMS ARE CHEAP, CLEAN, AND FRIENDLY!

A big-boned man waited just beyond the flags, facing away from the inn, hands clasping a long staff behind his back. His frame was so huge, Moonshadow decided, that at one time he might have been a professional wrestler. If that guess was right, if he was an ex-sumo, the stranger had lost a lot of weight since then. He now wore the robes of a town businessman. Moonshadow crossed the porch and the visitor turned as if hearing his approach.

"Ah, young sir! Forgive this intrusion. I am Katsu, freelance detective." The man bowed, a formal smile bending his long moustache. Moonshadow bowed back, regarding him warily. Good hearing, he thought, but no bladed weapons that were visible. And he admitted to being a private investigator! What was going on here?

"You seem familiar, sir," Moonshadow lied confidently. "Are you not a famous wrestler?"

The man's eyes momentarily lit up, then seemed to grow fixed and probing. Just as the innkeeper had warned!

"I once wrestled, but that was years ago. You would have been too young to see me fight." Katsu shrugged, grinning disarmingly. "Perhaps all sumo types are somewhat alike?"

This big man, Moonshadow decided, might prove to be quite dangerous. Cool natured and quick-witted, he should be responded to with care. The hasty question about wrestling had been a mistake. It had given the stranger his first insight into Moonshadow, that he was a good—maybe trained—observer. A pity he should have learned that so quickly.

Who had sent him? What was he really after?

"Forgive my rudeness. I meant no disrespect," Moonshadow said. "A detective, then? How exciting! But surely you can't be after a person like me?" He laughed, gesturing expansively. "No murderers here! Just a dull, hard-working messenger from Edo!"

"Indeed?" Katsu chuckled, too knowingly for Moonshadow's liking. "Well, in fact, my current case involves no murders. It's all about a hero, actually, not a villain. I have been knocking on doors inquiring of many a hard-working youth today." From his robe he yanked a patterned cloth purse. "You see, I seek a certain brave boy pilgrim. I've been hired by...let's just say by a pious client who wishes to remain anonymous."

"Hired to do what?"

"To honor this daring young man for his charity and valor. My client witnessed his chivalry near Hakone on the Tokaido, and says that Lord Buddha will not let him sleep until the boy is rewarded!" Katsu shook the purse, making its contents jingle. "Are you he, by any chance? I must observe, you are the right age and height and generally fit the description I have."

"As many do, I suppose," Moonshadow said casually. Katsu nodded and shrugged again.

For a split second, Moonshadow wondered if the girl had sent this Katsu. He quickly dismissed the thought. Her again! Why did he keep thinking of her? He forced himself to concentrate on the detective. This man—and his story—felt all wrong. Whoever he was, whatever he really wanted, he was no ally of the Grey Light.

Katsu's random movements, the vitality in his eyes, and his steady, silent breathing told Moonshadow three things: the detective was very physically strong, mentally sharp, and highly disciplined. He gave nothing else away, a warning in itself. Only a fool would trust him, for he was definitely a player in this game. But on whose side?

Badger had coached him in dealing with authorities like magistrates or the police. Don't just listen to their questions, the archivist had warned. Consider their unspoken strategy: where the questions are leading. They will try to trap you with your own answers, so choose each word with care. Any new facts you blurt will come back at you like *shuriken*. To mislead them, you must move, breathe, and even glance as one wholly innocent.

"I'm neither the hero you seek," Moonshadow stretched as if the whole matter was starting to bore him, "nor even a pilgrim!" He patted the calligraphy on his clothing. "Just a poor runner of messages between the eastern and western capitals."

"Hmm." Katsu nodded amiably. "And just arrived from Edo, you said?"

Moonshadow sensed the snare in his questioning. "I said from Edo, yes. But not just arrived. I've been in the area several days, delivering letters in both Otsu and Kyoto." He almost winced. That was too specific. He'd handed Katsu new "facts."

"Ah." Katsu's eyes shone. "I was in Kyoto myself last week. Along the road facing Nijo Castle, those hedges of *kirishima* flowers—you know, azaleas—are they not looking magnificent this spring? One type in particular... such an outstanding color."

"*Kirishima* flowers?" Moonshadow did his best impression of the stone Buddha outside the local temple. Katsu was watching his face closely. The smallest twitch would betray him.

"Yes, banks of them. One color seems to have taken over this year."

Moonshadow's gaze blankly drifted left and right before meeting Katsu's seeking stare. "What a shame I missed out on them. Sadly, my deliveries took me nowhere near the castle."

"Mmm." The detective's face hinted at a smile. "Indeed, a great pity." He bowed to Moonshadow.

"I apologize for wasting your time. A good day and a safe visit to you!" He turned and lumbered off down the street, swinging his staff, whistling.

Carefully Moonshadow watched him. Katsu never looked back.

"I haven't seen the last of you, have I?" Moonshadow muttered. This snoop's arrival was a bad development. Things had been going quite smoothly, but now he was under suspicion. Another day's scouting and preparation would have been ideal, but with Katsu prowling the town, the wisest course was to waste no time. What if the big man reappeared tomorrow with fifty local samurai at his back?

Moonshadow glanced toward the castle. Yes. He'd go in tonight.

He turned to cross the porch, then decided to quickly check for other potential threats. While pretending to inspect the porch flags, Moonshadow examined everyone in sight out of the corners of his eyes.

Other than the hulking form of Katsu, there were about twenty people on the street. By their faces or walks he was quickly able to eliminate each one from the category of possible problem. Soon only one remained. A flower-seller, fifty paces away, hunched over her tray of colorful *kirishima* flowers...the very azaleas of which Katsu had spoken. Heron was especially fond of azaleas. That unusual peasant girl probably liked them too....

"Why do I get so distracted lately?" Moonshadow whispered to himself. "If I don't watch that, I'll start making mistakes."

He quickly looked the flower-seller over. Her head was shrouded, face hidden, by a brightly colored scarf. Moonshadow watched her shoulders move as she sorted azaleas, studied the line of her slightly hunched back.

"No, too old." He returned to the inn. "No one I should worry about."

MIRROR IMAGE

Snowhawk looked up as the boy left the porch. She had felt his eyes glide over her. Now she was grateful that apparently, from the way he had just turned and disappeared, her disguise had fooled him. He'd believed her an old, hunched woman.

Her thorough training had proved itself again; it appeared she could deceive almost anyone.

Whoever he was, though, he was still pretty sharp. Snowhawk had watched him handle the nosy private detective. Even at this distance, it had been obvious that he had read the big man as easily as a scholar might discern a cheap, unreliable travel guidebook. Having had time now to study this boy, Snowhawk was convinced of a few things.

She had been right to return to this spot and watch for him after seeing him by chance down the street earlier, in his new disguise, striding from the inn. Regardless of that disguise, she had recognized him with absolute certainty. His balanced grace and his eyes had given him away. It was *him*: the same brave stranger who, dressed as a pilgrim, had rescued her and the farmers on the Great Road. Snowhawk gave a slightly smug grin. The gullible farmers she had used for travel cover. Why had he done it? Maybe he liked her. That could prove useful later on.

There should be no underestimating him, however. This quick-thinking boy had many skills. Subtle combat. Changing his appearance. Handling the suspicious interrogator now striding off down the street. The boy was clearly a professional.

But a *warrior monk*? Snowhawk laughed. His trainers might have included a few, perhaps, but no, he himself was no staff-carrying chanter. Her face tightened.

He was like her. He was *shinobi*. A spy, and clearly a gifted one.

Not perfect, though: he'd just failed to notice

her, right under his nose. Some spies were good at sensing each other's presence. He appeared under-developed in that area. She nodded. That too was worth remembering.

Watching him in action back on the highway had impressed her. He was an outstanding warrior, fast and agile. Snowhawk stared thoughtfully at the porch of the inn, at the exact spot where she had last seen him. In all likelihood, this boy was the male version of her. If that were so, then he too was here to get the plans.

Had the shadow clan *he* served perceived the same grand chance for profit as her masters? Did they too intend to steal, then secretly auction Silver Wolf's new asset among the faithless, opportunistic warlords? Perhaps. A creature like herself or not, that made him her rival.

Things could get complicated. Snowhawk sighed deeply. She would love to speak with the boy. He might be the first person she'd ever met who could understand her privileged, lonely life. The honor, the pride, and the *burden* of being *shinobi*. As her trainers said, one selected to do great deeds in secret, topple princes, and alter the course of history. One who did things others could not.

She closed her eyes. One destined to walk alone,

friendless and often fearful, never daring to fail. Who but her own kind would comprehend such a destiny?

Yes, he could very well be her mirror image. She hung her head. Mirror image or not, she might end up having to kill him.

TOOLS OF THE TRADE

For the remainder of the day, Moonshadow was uneasy, half-expecting Katsu to return leading Silver Wolf's men to the inn. As darkness fell, he dutifully recited the *furube* sutra and then placed a tiny iron wedge in the runner of his door, locking his room. He unpacked his equipment for the mission, spreading his gear out on the matting so he could check each individual piece.

Under his specially hued night suit, he would wear a full-body undergarment of thin wire mesh. The featherweight cousin of chain mail, it offered some protection from part-blunt or light blades. But if forced to deal with multiple guards at close quarters, he would need more protection than it gave. Moonshadow unfolded two strips of lightweight, segmented thigh armor, checking the ties on each strip's joints. The armor was unique to the Grey Light Order, each leg lined with a series of tough leather pouches. Flexible but strong, it reached hip to knee. Inspired by the shells of armadillos and insects, the leggings could deflect arrows or be used as shields when dueling. Moonshadow donned the mesh, then his night suit, and finally, the leg armor.

He examined each of his tools before stowing them in the leggings' pouches, distributing their combined weight evenly.

First, his pair of *shuko*, black iron climbing claws. Usually, the hand claws would be paired with *ashiko*, strap-on iron foot spikes, but those added extra weight. Moonshadow preferred serrated-sole sandals, which were much lighter. He checked that the *shuko*'s prongs were sound, leather palm straps intact. Once over the moat, these claws and the serrated grip of his specially woven sandals would help him scale the wall and gain entry to the castle through a drain outlet.

Moonshadow pulled on the draw cords of his night suit's thick, open-faced hood, tightening it around his head. Its interior was lined with a special red fabric, the color of which disguised blood. Should his neck or face be wounded, his enemies wouldn't know they had made him bleed. Even when soaked with blood, the unique red fabric simply looked wet, as if from sweat. Its use among spies had given rise to a predictable legend. Simple folk said that the men and women of the shadows had strange powers, for even when cut, these spies did not bleed. Guards who had fought *shinobi*, only to see them escape, apparently unharmed, had no doubt started such rumors.

Moonshadow knotted the hood's draw cords, then tied the end of his sash around his face to cover it. He wound the long indigo belt around his waist, then up over one shoulder, setting clever, open knots in it that could hold his sheathed sword on either his back or left hip. The knotted sash made it easy to move his weapon between the two locations, making a certain trick possible.

If facing a good swordsman, he could quickly switch his sword from back to hip, then perform a speed draw like a regular duelist. Most samurai guards attacking a spy would be unprepared for such a move, since *shinobi* usually wore their swords in back-mounted sheaths. Few would expect a lightning draw from the hip instead.

Mantis had shown him the trick, saying at the time with just a hint of bitterness, "It's a ploy that will surprise even experienced swordsmen. I should know; it worked on me the first time I saw it." He had then peeled open his jacket and shown his student a thin horizontal scar on his chest.

Into the leggings went Moonshadow's burglary tools: an iron right-angle for lifting heavy roof tiles without a sound, a small iron hook and a series of thin blades used for picking locks, a long, weighted, reinforced cord on a wooden spool, and water in a bamboo phial.

Moonshadow counted his stocks of *shuriken* and smoke bombs, then turned to his means of transport over the moat. From his pack he drew out eight quarter circles and two strong crossbeams fitted with foot straps, carved from a certain buoyant timber. He checked that the parts snapped together easily to form a pair of *mizu gumo* or "water spiders." First, the quarter-circles were assembled into two large discs, each held together with cunning, spring-loaded joints. Finally the two crossbeams and their leather straps were slotted in place wholly within each circle. Moonshadow tested the strength of the water spiders, then took them apart again and spread their parts throughout his legging pouches.

He smiled as he worked, recalling Ground-spider's many failed attempts to use the floating discs. Wearing them like great round shoes, a very light person—one with a typical *shinobi* build like Moonshadow—could balance upright on *mizu gumo* and cross a moat or still river. Being unusually big and solid for a spy, Groundspider would always flip upside-down then thrash about underwater, dangling from the strapped-on floats like a huge drowning bat.

Despite fleeting moments of nervousness at his looming task, Moonshadow chuckled, picturing Groundspider, drenched to the bone and taking his *mizu gumo* apart, after a failed moat crossing near the shogun's fortress in Edo. "What are *you* smirking at, kid?" The big fellow had said, scowling with mock menace. "I'm better than you at everything else! Besides, this keeps happening only because I'm a *ground* spider!"

At last Moonshadow fed his short, straight *shinobi* sword into the knots waiting on his back, slinging beside it the cloth pack that held his day clothes. With his equipment in place, he unlocked the door. He waited awhile, listening carefully to the night sounds of the inn, until satisfied that everyone else was sleeping and no one lurked in the corridor between his room and the rear exit. He opened his door, crept unchallenged from the building, and moved through the town's narrow back alleys for the castle.

The midnight bell hummed from Fushimi's largest temple, its deep ring turning butterflies loose in his stomach. Moonshadow crouched in shadow, scanning the front stretch of Momoyama Castle's moat. His hand slid to his belly, trying to calm its writhing. What was wrong with him?

As he realized, Moonshadow sighed heavily.

He was confident he could cross that water, enter the castle.

But suddenly he doubted that he'd make it out again.

15

TO CROSS THE MOAT

Though the night was ink-black, Moonshadow knew the real moon would rise all too soon from behind the distant mountains, a glowing crescent that would flood the rooftops with a dangerous amount of light. He had to stay ahead of that moonrise, or at the very least be on his way out of the castle when it struck.

Moonshadow passed the temple and crept along the moat's shadowy bank, dotted on the town side with willow trees and lone, twisted pines. His dark blue-purple night suit gave him confidence, for he knew its unique color was harder to distinguish in shadow or half-light than plain black. But the first hint of real fear was already gnawing at the edges of his mind.

This was no training exercise. This was real: life and death. It was time to take control *within* through reciting the *furube* sutra, not dutifully as he did each dawn and sunset, but almost *desperately*, for now he faced real action.

Furube meant to shake or shrug something off. This "shaking off" ritual made spies ready to carry out their missions. It cleared the mind, sharpened the senses, and helped a *shinobi* throw off all distractions before going about his work. It also reminded him to heed the consequences of his actions, since even a warrior with special powers created good or bad *karma* with every choice he made.

In the darkness at the base of a tree, Moonshadow folded his legs and sat on his heels. He narrowed his eyes and whispered the sutra's three verses, bringing his palms together, folding and unfolding his fingers, forming a different knot or symbol to accompany each line of the sutra.

As Mantis had said repeatedly, the phrase "scatter not one grain of life" meant, among other things, *never kill if you have a choice*.

It had been hard to believe that this pious man, despite his incredible skills, had ever killed anyone, until Eagle had revealed that Brother Mantis, "in the wildness of his youth," had dueled for a living, killing seventy-five men in single combat.

Moonshadow drew a slow breath. Would he be forced to kill tonight?

He widened his eyes. He looked around, took in the moat, the distant bridge across it, the sloping castle walls beyond. He was having real trouble readying his mind. What was wrong with him? The *furube* had done half its work, for that initial sliver of fear had faded away. No, it wasn't that.

Moonshadow shook his head as he realized. He was thinking of that girl again. Was he somehow sensing her nearby? This was happening too often. He scowled. She should leave town. Girls were a nuisance! He narrowed his eyes and recited the sutra again, forcing himself to concentrate harder.

At last the awareness of her also faded, replaced by increasing clarity. His mind grew orderly, an undisturbed pond. He opened his eyes wide and looked up at the walls, beyond which his prize waited. His goal was everything now. Moonshadow was tranquil but alert. Ready, eager, and more than that, *fearless*.

He kept his breathing even as he stood up and stretched. The banks of the moat were quiet, but a splash made him turn. Moonshadow listened, his eyes moving back and forth over the water. There! Giant carp were nosing the surface not far from the bank. They dived skittishly with more splashing, becoming long grey shadows for an instant before they vanished.

Murmuring drifted across the water. Guards' voices. Moonshadow heard another carp splash in the moat as it took a swimming insect. He frowned hard. Light as *he* was, if just one of those great fish nudged his water spiders, he would flip over like Groundspider and hang in extreme peril. As he watched he realized that the moat teemed with carp, many of them the length and girth of his leg.

He glanced at the top of the curved wall. A faint glow above the massive stones marked a guard post's cooking fire. Silver Wolf's confident, aggressive men at the Hakone Barrier were amateurs compared with what he could expect here in Fushimi. These castle samurai, charged with protecting their master, would be the best of the warlord's fighters. If he was detected and forced to engage them, he'd be up against men chosen not only for their strength and speed, but for their willingness to lay down their lives for their liege lord. He felt his chest tighten in anticipation.

Moonshadow stared down at the moat, smelling its water and mud. If he capsized out there he had two choices, both of them nasty. He could dangle silently until his held breath ran out and he drowned. Or he could free himself of the floats and swim away frantically, a noisy process on a still night like this. He lifted his eyes to the castle. If *that* happened, no matter how far he swam submerged, dozens of arrows would fly from the top of that wall, probing the moat relentlessly until they found him.

Perhaps that glow wasn't really a cooking fire. Maybe the castle was on high alert already, and the guards were prepared to launch fire arrows at the first suspicious sound they heard. He felt his breath quicken. Fire arrows were a *triple* hazard. They broke the darkness, neutralizing night suits. If their tips were bound with oiled cloth, they could even carry light a short distance underwater, revealing a submerged intruder. Worst of all, if they actually pierced their intended target while still burning…

He forced that image from his mind. Moonshadow crept into the shadows of a willow overhanging the moat. At the very edge he assembled and fitted the water spiders, then used dangling branches to help him stand and stabilize himself. As he released the willow branches, Moonshadow glanced down at his hands. His fingertips were trembling.

Once he felt in control of the bobbing floats, Moonshadow slowed his breathing again and began taking the long, rhythmic strides that would propel him out over the water. He moved through the darkest shadows, careful not to be seen. Throughout his training, Moonshadow had practically lived on steamed vegetables and fruits, coated in a potion of ginseng and mountain country herbs that increased the flow of blood to his eyes. The special diet had given him exceptional night vision. By the time he was halfway across the moat, he could make out fine details on the castle wall.

Torches atop the huge stones lit up the moat with fingers of light. Moonshadow zigzagged forward slowly, keeping to the darkest shadows, arms outstretched at either side as he padded along uneasily on the water. Each wooden float hovered and slid just under the surface. Cold water stung through his sandals and the split-toed cotton boots beneath them. Soon his toes were numb and the chill was climbing up through his ankles. Walking on water was nerve-wracking and awkward, but the technique worked. Trying not to become tense, Moonshadow silently mouthed comforting words: *If only Ground-spider could see this.*

He neared the curved, damp wall and made for his target: a small drain outlet breaking the smooth stones roughly ten paces above the moat. A thin stream of water ran from it constantly, making the stones below it shine. It was a narrow duct. The *shuko*, his claws, and the grip of his sandals should get him up there, but then would come the hard part. The painful part.

To fit into that drain, he would need to dislocate his left shoulder. If he could manage that tonight as well as he had in training, he could slide through the castle's under-floor drains to the kitchen or laundry. According to Badger's charts of Momoyama Castle, this particular drain outlet did *not* come from the latrines.

But what if that was a mistake? He nearly shuddered at the idea. If only he could be sure Badger's charts were unspoiled and accurate! There was a risk that the crucial brushstroke he was relying on had actually been a streak of monkey's dung.

He heard some guards bantering, the sounds of a fire being stoked, more general bustle suggesting a large group of men further along the wall. Why so many on the walls tonight? His heart skipped a beat at the thought that he might be expected. So many samurai up there. What if he *was* caught?

Moonshadow had heard what warlords did to spies and would-be assassins caught within their castles. Yes, they were executed ... *eventually*. First, patient attempts were made to learn who they served, who had trained them, what their objectives were.

Thoughts of how this information was extracted made his blood run cold.

Moonshadow concentrated on the drain. It was dead ahead now, quite close, but a strip of well-lit water lay between him and the dim wall beneath it. He stopped, still in shadow, looking up, hovering as he weighed the problem facing him.

A high parapet overlooked his escape route and, from time to time, voices came from it. Moonshadow shook his head. Great stones beside the observation niche blocked his view into it. Was the parapet empty now or not? There could be guards up there, watching in silence. If so, once he moved forward into that brighter patch of water, he'd be seen. Quickly thereafter, he'd wish he were dead.

He had to make a decision. If the parapet *was* empty right now, he was already wasting valuable time. If he bobbed around out here for too long, the moon would rise and make him a target even a one-eyed archer could hit. Moonshadow glanced in all directions. Forward now, or not? Moonshadow bit his lip, ordering himself to *stay calm*. But calm was escaping him now. A huge carp noisily broke the surface to his left. Great! This was all he needed…an oversized fish to draw attention to him, even in the shadows! At least there was only one.

Another splash. He looked about quickly. A huge school of giant carp was surfacing all around him, perhaps curious about his water spiders. What if their splashing made the guards investigate? What if, any second, one of these stupid fish tipped him over? He silently scolded himself for panicking. At least they weren't rising under his feet. Then a huge white carp broke the surface sharply, right between his floats. "No," Moonshadow gasped, swaying on the spot. "Go away," he hissed.

His frightened eyes widened at the big fish. One flick of its tail and over he'd go!

DREAM OF DRAGONS

Heron knelt alone on a reed mat in the monastery's small kitchen, staring into the teacup between her palms. The kitchen door slid open behind her. She turned to it.

"So." Eagle nodded. "It *was* you I heard. Such light steps. For a moment there, I wondered if a skilled intruder was loose within our walls..." He scratched his neck and muttered, "...if my time had finally come."

"Forgive me," Heron said, returning her gaze to the steam rising from her tea.

"Did it happen again?" Eagle knelt down beside her. "Another prophetic dream?"

She looked at him anxiously. "I saw Moonshadow. I saw him standing, balancing on the white-capped waves of a raging sea, dragons rising all around him. Yet he crosses no oceans on his mission. What could the image mean?"

Brother Eagle shook his head. "Who can say? But the White Nun warned you last year, when you began the lessons with her, did she not? What were her words? Until long into the training, you would foresee *true nonsense*: a mix of fact and lies."

"Yes. As if inks of two different colors had spilled together."

Eagle smiled tenderly. "Don't let the murky result scare you."

"But the White Nun also bade me take careful note of what I sensed on waking, remember? Those impressions, the strings of words, have always been far clearer."

Eagle gave a single nod. "Indeed. Those riddle-phrases of yours, as I have called them…it's true that so far, as best we can judge them, they *have* come to pass. So what strange words came to you this dark morning? Were they also about our young Moonshadow?"

"Yes." Heron gave him a frightened glance. "As I woke, this formed in my mind: *He will not return, or he'll return with another prize. One for which he'll bleed.*"

"How confusing." Eagle huffed in frustration. "Does it mean that if he survives, he'll bring back something other than the prize we sent him after? Or that he'll fetch the plans *and* some further asset Silver Wolf hoards, one we don't know about?"

Heron shrugged. "I'm sorry, but I have no idea. In poison, smoke, or pole-blade, I am the assured teacher. In matters of *this* science, though, I am but a floundering student." She fixed Eagle with a pleading stare. "But I fear for him, how I fear for him now!"

Eagle reached out and, with the back of his hand, gently brushed her cheek. "Then even though your latest riddle is a tangled forest indeed, I shall act on it."

"How?" Her face brightened. "What can you do?"

"Groundspider left with orders to collect three other field agents and then meet the boy when his mission was done. In the light of your—*our*—new concerns, I'll dispatch a rider to our safe inn on the Tokaido near Fushimi. He'll carry coded orders for Groundspider to double the number of men who'll escort Moonshadow home."

Heron's eyes gleamed as she held back tears. "You doubt me less than I doubt myself." She smiled. "Thank you!"

Eagle shrugged. "After all, we might *need* several agents to help carry this other prize." His face suddenly darkened and he shook his head. "Let's just pray it doesn't turn out to be something like the warlord's pet tiger."

EYE OF THE BEAST

The white carp dived again, but the danger wasn't over. Moonshadow bobbed on the moat, watching in horror as still more giant carp rose and surrounded him. The largest, an enormous black-and-white speckled female, closed in and sniffed his water spider foot floats, apparently trying to decide if they were a potential meal.

"No," Moonshadow whispered desperately. "These spiders you can't eat."

His heart raced but he dared not move. From the wall above, the words of a guard reached him. They were surprisingly clear. The man was complaining about how much he wanted to kill someone called Jiro.

"Oi!" A guard with a much deeper voice cut his colleague off. "Get in line," the man said gruffly. "My sword saw his neck first!"

Then a third fellow spoke, dropping a name that made Moonshadow's heart pound even harder.

"Ah, that Jiro's nothing. Forget his throwing-knife tricks! Gangster trash!" The tone of the man's voice abruptly shifted. "It's the third one that makes my skin crawl. The Deathless...huh! They should call him The Bloodless. At least he's on *our* side!"

"You know what one of the maids told me?" the first guard piped up. "She saw The Deathless loosen his hood so he could eat. She said he has the head of a great owl!"

There were murmurs of awe from the other two, then the deep-voiced guard said quickly, "Enough! We shouldn't be speaking of him. He could be anywhere...listening!"

The three fell silent.

Below them, Moonshadow found his thoughts racing to catch up with his heart. The Deathless? And he could be anywhere? It sounded as if Silver Wolf had turned him loose, like a roving guard dog, to wander the castle's grounds. He cast a nervous look back at the banks of the moat. Nothing. But of course such a foe wouldn't show himself before striking.

He glanced down. Carp steadily circled his water spiders. Moonshadow swallowed hard, hoping they would lose interest and move along. But he had more than idiot fish to worry about now. Could it be true? Was The Deathless himself working for Silver Wolf?

This was very bad news! Every *shinobi* in Japan had heard of the supposedly unkillable assassin. It was widely whispered that The Deathless was no myth. That he truly deserved his title. That he had mastered that most difficult and ancient of Old Country sciences: immunity to the blade of a sword. Heron herself had told Moonshadow, over a year ago, that there really was such a lost art, though nobody in the Grey Light Order understood it.

A fat carp passed within a hand's width of his left float. Moonshadow held his breath. It turned away, then dived without bumping the bobbing wood. That title was ringing in his head now. *The Deathless*. What else did he know about the legendary assassin?

Within the spy community, it was said that only one other man had the same uncanny power: Koga Danjo himself, ninja master and trainer of

The Deathless. But a rumor had gone around, a few months back, that The Deathless had murdered his legendary teacher. If that was true, The Deathless alone now possessed his secrets.

The remaining carp circled Moonshadow a last time then moved away. He sighed with relief as he watched them drift toward the bank until they again began to circle, this time in a finger of light that crossed the moat from a burning torch on top of the wall.

Now directly in line with the observation parapet but farther away from it than Moonshadow, the great fish started feeding off water boatmen and other insects teeming in one area.

Moonshadow wrenched The Deathless from his mind and glanced between the carp and the parapet. The speckled one kept breaking the water, its round, shiny head facing the castle walls. That dumb fish, he thought bitterly, had a better-angled view of the parapet than he did.

An idea came to him. Using the eye of the beast, *his* Old Country science, he could look through that carp's eyes and learn if the parapet was empty or not. Then he would know whether to move forward or wait. A fine solution, but of course, there was a catch.

To maintain a basic sight-joining, he had to close his eyes. That was fine while hovering, but once he moved forward, with his eyes shut, he would be unable to control his balance. It was hard enough balancing on water with his eyes open!

Moonshadow would have to take an even greater risk and try something *new*. He had tried to practice this on the road to Fushimi, but that chance had been dangerously interrupted. Now he *had to* make it work.

Beyond mere, basic beast sight lay two higher stages. Moonshadow gave a purposeful nod. Tonight, he would have to operate on the *second* level: dual sight. He needed to see through that carp, but use his own eyes too. He'd tried for dual sight before, but only during training, or as a personal challenge. Now he must do it here, with everything at stake, *and* make it last.

The speckled carp broke the surface, facing the parapet once more. He closed his eyes and concentrated on it. His hands trembled as vague snatches of the fish's vision appeared, distorted through what looked like two quivering layers of water. The first layer was real, the water of the moat. The second veil was a regular symptom of the joining he was used to seeing. Moonshadow breathed in, preparing to open his eyes while holding the beast sight in his mind. His heart beat like a war drum in his chest. He opened one eye. The beast sight vanished. Moonshadow cursed under his breath, closed his eyes, and started again. The vision would not come. Eagle's words rang in his anxious mind. *To do the impossible, you must first stop caring about the outcome.* Fear of failure was blocking his powers. Moonshadow opened both eyes, cleared his mind, and recited the *furube* again.

"Anyway," a guard's voice abruptly rang from somewhere above, "I'll bet you three copper coins that The Deathless ends up killing Jiro for us!" Laughter followed.

"You're on, you're on!" a man with a high, squeaky voice replied. Moonshadow heard coins jingling. More laughter followed.

"I will not fear failure, just as I will not fail," Moonshadow whispered. He doggedly repeated the sutra again, and at last regained his calm.

Now he was ready. He closed his eyes and linked his mind to the carp's again. Taking his time, he watched the watery beast sight images change and distort for a while, then, with a new sense of confidence, he opened both eyes.

He saw the castle wall and the drain ahead of him

with his own sight. Superimposed over it, he saw a different, higher section of the wall at the same time. That image was bending and stretching constantly yet was clear enough for him to make out details.

Moonshadow could see into the mouth of the parapet now. Two guards, one with a spear over his shoulder, were turning and leaving it. A wave of weariness swept through him. Eagle had warned him about this: the highest levels of the gift were demanding. They sucked the *ki* energy, the life force, from their operator, so should be used sparingly. Moonshadow blinked, watching the parapet distort through rippling water. The stone niche was still empty.

Moonshadow gritted his teeth and strode forward to cross the finger of light. As he entered it, a warning instinct made his skin prickle.

He glanced quickly along the battlements. All was quiet up there now. No movement. "Stop imagining things," Moonshadow mumbled, taking another wary stride.

The instinct clutched at him again, forming itself into words.

Hostile eyes watch you!

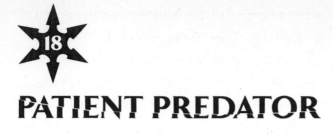

PATIENT PREDATOR

On the town side of the moat, high up on the largest temple's shadowy roof, The Deathless raised a European spyglass to one eye. He gently pulled on the widest end of the segmented cylinder until the spyglass's round, dim image grew sharp.

The Deathless grinned as he watched Moonshadow slowly cross the well-lit strip of water. He swung the spyglass up, then left and right. The nearest parapet was empty, the closest guards on the wall unaware of the invader's presence. He lowered the spyglass and nodded.

"How did you time that so well? You must have talents, runt," The Deathless muttered. "But gifted or not, in this world you are still the dove and I the falcon." He raised the instrument to his eye again. The unknown spy had now reached the shadowy base of the wall, directly below a drain outlet.

Like Moonshadow, The Deathless had been reared to see in darkness that left normal men blind. His vision penetrated the haze. He watched the slender intruder cling to the wall like a frog, peel off a pair of water spiders, and slowly feed their parts, one at a time, into his leggings. The figure then rummaged for something else in his hidden pockets, hunched against the wall, head turning warily in all directions.

"What do you fish for?" The Deathless whispered. "Rope and grappler?" A moment later the slim, dark outline was on the move, steadily climbing for the drain outlet. The assassin nodded again. The way this agent spread himself flat, quickly securing good hand- and footholds, suggested the skillful use of climbing claws.

"Yes, real talent." The Deathless chuckled. "But it will not be enough. I will wait, poised to strike at your worst possible moment. And once I discover where your limits lie..."

He closed his spyglass with a muffled *snap*.

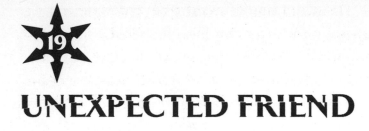

UNEXPECTED FRIEND

Moonshadow hung with one hand from the drain's protruding stone mouth, packing away his second climbing claw with the other. After breaking the sight-joining, he had felt confused as usual, but this time the mental fuzziness seemed to be lasting longer. A thin stream of water fell beside him from the drain. It didn't smell too bad, so Moonshadow leaned forward and passed his hooded head under the small cascade. The shock of the cold water cleared his mind a little, but he knew he could not wait for every trace of the joining to disperse. All too soon, that moon would rise.

He hauled himself up and crouched on the trough-shaped outlet, working his left shoulder loose. He prepared himself for pain, placed his right fist under his left armpit, and steadily forced the shoulder from its socket. There was a loud, nauseating *click.* Moonshadow almost bit his tongue as he stifled an agonized gasp.

His eyes watered and his teeth ground together. At first it felt as if his arm were on fire and being torn from his body. Then the awful pain settled down to a dull, constant throbbing. Moonshadow angled his right shoulder forward, tucked in his chin, and fed himself into the drain headfirst. Moonshadow inchwormed along on his belly through a thin layer of water, his dislocated arm trailing, rubbing against the drain's stone side. There was a dull *thud*, then what sounded like a heavy gate creaking shut somewhere above him. He froze, looking up, listening anxiously.

If he was detected in here, he would be defenseless. Groundspider had told him of a *shinobi* once trapped in a similar drain. That man's enemies had poured oil into the narrow tunnel, then set it alight. The desperate spy had barely escaped with his life, diving—on fire—into the moat and sustaining terrible burns.

From overhead, nothing but silence now. He moved on, listening warily.

When he had traveled about sixty paces in the dark, cramped channel, he smelled wet fur up ahead. An animal. A rat, maybe. If Badger's chart of the castle was accurate and Moonshadow's estimate of how far he had come was also correct, he was now under the great courtyard. The outer mansions, guard quarters, and landscaped gardens were all behind him now. Ahead loomed the central tower of the castle complex. At its base were living areas, stables, and kitchens, and above them, its master's rooms and audience chamber. And, most importantly, at the very top of the keep, his treasure vault.

The drain grew lighter as he pressed forward and suddenly he could see the silhouette of a creature in his path. Its pointy ears brushed against the drain's ceiling. Moonshadow slid forward, straining his eyes at the animal until he could tell what it was.

It was a lean cat, the type known as a kimono cat, contentedly chewing on a rat it had already beheaded. Just past it, the drain widened, becoming brighter still. Moonshadow reached the feeding animal. It gave him a curious look, then turned and scuttled ahead, the rat hanging from its mouth. Moonshadow frowned. This cat was odd! The black-and-white pattern on its back resembled a woman wearing a kimono, a traditional Japanese robe, hence the name kimono cat. Cats born with these mark-ings were considered sacred and sent to live on the grounds of temples, so they were also called temple cats. But this one was like no other he had seen: it had a long tail. The tail of a temple cat was normally short, broad, and almost triangular in shape.

"You're different. A loner like me, huh?" Moon-shadow whispered to the cat.

It stopped and looked back at him, then gave a muffled *meow* as if agreeing. He winced. Its cry might draw attention. The cat scurried ahead until it stopped beneath an iron grate. Moonshadow lis-tened carefully and sampled the dank air before catch-ing up to the animal. Old smells of soy sauce, spilled sake, and burned rice told him they had reached a kitchen at the base of the keep. His sharp ears said it was unoccupied right now.

Lantern or candlelight streamed in from the iron grate and Moonshadow dragged himself cautiously under it. The bars were just far enough apart for him to squeeze through the grate without a dislo-cated shoulder. Moonshadow had just enough room now to rise to his knees and reach across his body for his dangling left arm. Once more he prepared for pain. The cat tilted its head, watching his every move intently.

With a dull *snap* he put his shoulder back in its socket. The cat flinched at the sound, dropped its rat, and sprang up through the grate. Wiping tears of pain from his eyes, Moonshadow clambered slowly after it. He rose to his feet and gingerly stretched. He was inside the kitchen's storeroom, not the kitchen itself. The cat stared at him, tail swishing.

His shoulder throbbed but his mind had cleared now from the effects of the carp-joining, and his internal strength and energy were returning. A good thing, he decided. He was going to need them.

The storeroom was shadowy like the kitchen beyond it. Both were lit by a series of well-spaced iron lanterns. Moonshadow heard a faint *sniff*. In the nearby corridor lurked the first of many night watch guards. Vigilant, handpicked samurai, each one armed with two swords.

He slid off his cloth pack and emptied it. Tightly folding his day clothes and the pack itself, he distributed them throughout the pockets of his armored leggings. Now, with only his sword on his back, there was less for an enemy to snatch at.

He wedged himself into a dark corner and stared at the temple cat, which sat brushing its whiskers with its paw near the half-open sliding door to the kitchen. He would use it to scout before moving, but only on the least demanding level to conserve energy.

Moonshadow closed his eyes. His hands trembled. The cat sat bolt upright and, turning its head, stared at him. For the first time ever, he saw his own face through an animal's eyes. The usual shimmering, watery veil was there, but his features were distinct despite it, and the experience of seeing them was strange and unsettling.

He opened his dormant human eyes. Through the cat's sharp vision he saw an unexpected color glinting above his own high cheekbones. Now, while joined to this animal, the pupils of his unused eyes glowed with a subtle green hue. Did that always happen? Moonshadow watched himself frown as an odd, sharp taste grew strong in his mouth—which he hoped was not the taste of fresh rat's head—and the kitchen smells suddenly became almost overpowering.

The temple cat turned away and bounded through the half-open sliding door, eager to resume its rounds. Moonshadow watched carefully, taking in everything the creature saw as it padded around the kitchen looking for food.

Its vision lit on the paper-lined wall and the shadow of a corridor guard, standing tall and silent just outside. The cat vaulted onto a long bench, avoided a fish knife lying on it, then leapt to a large iron cooking plate set against the wall and framed by an archway of stones. Hunching in the center of the plate, the cat looked around before turning its gaze up. Moonshadow nodded at what he and the cat saw.

A rounded brick chimney, installed for cooking smoke to escape the kitchen, loomed above the plate. It had no bars, mesh, or bends, and was large enough for Moonshadow to ascend inside it. It had to emerge on a rooftop. But he didn't recall a chimney on Badger's chart. Was this new? If so, what else had recently changed? Just one new extra-tough door, unexpected grill, or new set of bars could destroy his mission.

The guard outside coughed, then groaned softly as he stretched. Through the cat, Moonshadow watched the man's shadow. He paced around a little circle near the kitchen door. He cleared his throat and spat into what looked like a small paper handkerchief. The cat and Moonshadow together saw the shadow of his head turn sharply toward the kitchen.

Was the guard about to sneak in for a cup of water? It was time to go!

Moonshadow broke the link with the cat and crept quickly along the ground, through the half-open sliding door and into the kitchen itself. The cat jumped from the cooking plate, following some promising smell with a twitching nose.

Moonshadow scrambled like a giant spider up onto the cooking plate and under the chimney. Watching the guard's silhouette with his own eyes now, he rummaged quickly for the climbing claws.

The guard moved for the kitchen. Moonshadow slid his hands into the claws. The guard gripped the paper screen door. As it rattled faintly, starting to open, Moonshadow fed his hands, then his head and shoulders up into the chimney, stabbing outwards with the claws for a pair of handholds. The outer door slid open and the guard stole into the kitchen, looking around for a cup. An instant before his roving gaze lit on the cooking plate, Moonshadow's legs disappeared up the chimney.

Moonshadow ascended with silent speed inside the long smokestack, the prongs of his claws finding thin gaps between each layer of bricks. Legs splayed, feet wedged against opposite walls, he climbed higher, listening to the sounds of the guard below him in the kitchen. They echoed, growing fainter. More coughing. The trickle of water leaving a jug. The guard grumbling to himself as he sat drinking on the edge of the cooking plate. Moonshadow glanced down. That was close!

The chimney emerged onto a gently sloping rain roof halfway up the side of the central tower, its opening covered with a small tiled roof of its own. Moonshadow squeezed himself from the chimney, rotated his aching left shoulder, then resumed climbing.

Now he moved under a crisp, starry sky. Cold night air stung his eyes as he clawed his way up massive stones and wooden beams to the top of Silver Wolf's tower. At last his claws *chinked* on the tiles of the keep's highest roof. Moonshadow paused to catch his breath, looking out over the castle.

Tall and thin, the keep stood alone in the center of a rectangle formed by the castle's outer buildings and their roofs, beyond which lay the walls, then the moat.

That outer rectangle and the keep were connected above ground level, but only at one point. A wide walkway, a miniature bridge, ran from the rain roof, where his surprise chimney had ended, across to one corner of the outer rectangle.

The walkway was obviously an archers' platform. From it, a regiment of shooters could defend the keep should the castle's outer defenses fall. He studied its design. If a desperate last stand by the archers failed, there were great ropes at the rain roof end that could be cut, dropping the platform, severing it from the keep so an invader couldn't use it. Moonshadow took off his claws as he watched the walkway. It looked empty, unguarded, but since Silver Wolf was no fool, it would be watched.

He glanced at the faint lights of the town, then took in more of the castle's layout. The walkway led to that same corner of the outer rectangle from which a cable ran across the moat to the sake brewery.

Moonshadow looked around. Would he see the cat again? He was tenser now than ever, and its presence had been strangely comforting, his link with it unusually strong. But the roof remained still, silent. The creature had gone on its way. Moonshadow steadied his breathing as best he could, stowed his iron claws, and stared down at the roof tiles under his feet. This was it! He recalled Eagle's final words to him in Edo.

Never forget your valuable place in the universe. To be trained as one of the shogun's shinobi, *to risk or even lose your life in his service...there can be no greater honor.* The real test of that training was about to begin. It was time to earn the honor—and the trust—afforded him. His stomach writhed; his heart pounded. He forced the fear from his thoughts.

According to Grey Light Order intelligence, the plans were right under his nose now, or rather, beneath his sandals. To be precise, they waited in the keep's uppermost chamber, locked in an ornate Chinese chest beside a much larger iron treasure vault. That greater, more enticing safe was simply a ruse, a false target designed to divert any would-be thief. Moonshadow wondered at the daring of the Grey Light Order infiltrator who had furnished them with such detailed information. Just before leaving Edo, Eagle had spoken—with great admiration—of this gifted field agent. He'd said only that they owed much to a woman, a former orphan like Moonshadow, who had served in the castle before faking her own drowning in the moat.

Moonshadow drew the tile-lifting tool from his leggings and, using it adeptly, pried two great roof tiles up and out of their wooden frames. He set them close to the hole he had created, balancing one on the other so that, if pursued up through the hole on his return, a gentle push would collapse the tiles onto his first pursuer's head.

He carefully swung his feet into the black cavity between roof and ceiling, about to descend. Out of the corner of one eye, an alarming detail caught his attention. He turned his head, making sure his impression was right. It was! A bead of nervous sweat glided down his spine. The sky to the east was growing lighter. The crescent moon was about to rise. He looked desperately from the black cavity to the sky and back again. His mind raced with calculations.

Moonshadow cursed. Getting in had taken too long. So, on the way out, strong moonlight would carve up the shadows, neutralize his night suit.

Every warrior in this castle would be able to see him!

THE PRIZE

Once inside the roof cavity, Moonshadow pressed an ear to the ceiling boards. He listened hard for sounds of life in the treasure room below. Nothing.

Moonshadow drew the burglary tools from his leggings. Using the thin blades, he silently popped one wooden ceiling square and slid it to one side. He dangled his head through the opening, letting his eyes adjust to the dim light of the room. A candle in an iron holder burned in the center of the polished hardwood floor. Another glowed between the only two pieces of furniture he could see: a fancy wooden

Chinese chest and a much larger, plainer safe of rough black metal beside it. Each had built-in locks, each a large keyhole. They stood together under the room's only window, which was shuttered and bolted.

It all looked just as Grey Light Order intelligence had predicted. Moonshadow sighed softly. It also looked too easy to be true.

He took the reinforced cord on the wooden spool from a pocket of his leggings. Moonshadow unwound the cord, then lowered its weighted end slowly until it touched the floor. Controlling the line with feather-light pressure, he gently dragged the weight across one floor plank and onto the next. When it had crossed several polished boards, the weight stopped moving freely and Moonshadow, sampling the cord's tension with his index finger, felt it snag. His eyes followed the cord down to the floor, hunting for whatever had trapped it. There it was, just as he had suspected, hiding in the shadows below the candles' glow.

A black wire cable, in fact several thin cables, crossed the floor a hand's width above the boards. They were designed to catch the feet of anyone moving from the reinforced sliding door to the window area. He hung upside down from the gap in the ceiling, turning his head, following the cables. At each end, they were connected to large bamboo chimes that hung in shadow. He set his jaw. There must be a guard—or several—just outside, ready to charge in at the slightest sound from those alarms.

Moonshadow retrieved his sensing cord, then pulled himself up and crept through the roof cavity until he was directly above the Chinese chest. He raised and discarded another wooden square. After judging the distance to the chest below, Moonshadow lowered himself over it. He hung by his fingertips from the edge of the hole he'd made, checked the rest of the room again, then soundlessly dropped to the chest.

On most missions, he would put out the candles before striking, lowering the sensing cord's weight above their flames and running drops of water down the cord. In this particular situation, that light was an ally he needed. He needed to see the cables of the chime traps at all times. He needed to verify the plans before he fled with them, in case Silver Wolf was using a second ruse: dummy plans. At least he'd been prepared. Thanks to Badger, Moonshadow knew exactly what to look for when he examined the documents, how to confirm their authenticity.

He crouched on the chest, too wary of more hidden traps to stand on any part of the floor itself. The very boards might be planed to rub against each other and sing like nightingales, bringing the guards—and death—down on him in the sweetest voice. He recalled Badger's detailed account of an ingenious alarm-floor in the inner corridor of mighty Nijo Castle, where recently a Grey Light agent had sustained mortal wounds after the boards sang beneath the weight of his feet. Leaning forward, working upside down with his small iron hook and thin blades, Moonshadow attacked the built-in lock on the Chinese chest.

When a soft *click* announced that he had beaten the mechanism, he stepped from the lid of the chest and clung to the side of the black iron vault that stood next to it. With one foot, Moonshadow swung the chest open. As its lid rose, there was a faint hiss and a spring-loaded blade shot up from inside the camphor-scented box. Moonshadow closed his eyes gratefully. If he'd been sloppy and careless, standing on the floor and looming unwisely over that chest, the blade now gleaming there would have sliced off his chin.

Still gripping the side of the vault, he leaned out, hovering above the open Chinese chest. Using the iron hook, Moonshadow fished out the chest's only contents apart from the spring-loaded blade trap. It was a plugged tube of polished bamboo, hung from a tough leather thong. Swinging from his burglary hook, it dangled in front of his eyes. Was this the real thing? The packaging looked right.

He needed somewhere to stand so he could use both hands while he checked the plans over. Using one foot, Moonshadow slowly closed the Chinese chest. The spring-loaded blade retracted, automatically folding, and the trap reset itself with a subtle double *click* as the lid came down. He nodded. Should these plans prove to be fake, he would open the chest again and replace them. Moonshadow stretched, stepping back onto the lid of the chest. He steadied his breathing once more and stowed his tools in his leggings.

Leaning out to catch the light of the candle, he unstopped the bamboo tube. Gently he pulled a single roll of handmade paper from it.

Moonshadow unwound the plans and looked them over. At once, every instinct told him they were the real thing. A series of technical drawings, with captions in some alien language, showed a peculiar device. It was similar to a musket, though part of its middle, near the trigger assembly, flared out like a water gourd. Lower on the page, a cutaway diagram of the flared section revealed six separate chambers inside it. Each chamber held its own lead ball, shot wad, and gunpowder. A set of cogs at either end meant this gourd-like magazine could be rotated, lining the weapon's barrel up first with one chamber, then with the next.

At the bottom of the single sheet, the plans carried an odd stamp mark Moonshadow had been told to look out for, the trademark of the black market broker Silver Wolf had used. So these *were* the real plans.

Moonshadow swallowed. He had known that his mission was to intercept plans for a weapon that would give Silver Wolf a tremendous advantage—an unacceptable advantage in the hands of one plotting rebellion. But *what* a weapon! Now, confronted with its details, the implications of this terrible device shocked him.

Warfare, the ancient craft of Japan's ruling class, would never be the same again. Every soldier toting a gun like this would get six shots, in rapid succession, before needing to reload it. That was enough firepower to bring down charging cavalry or rows of armored men. He shook his head, picturing a long line of such shooters. Then he imagined a whole army of them.

This weapon would dictate who ruled the country. Skill in combat would lose all importance, and what about rules of honor on the battlefield? The old way was to pick your opponent, declare your name, make a challenge, and duel him! It took courage to see a man's eyes as you fought him up close.

To fire on a distant, faceless foe, no manners, honor, or courage would be required. Silver Wolf not only intended to plunge the country back into war. He would bring *future war*, using an ugly new science Japan had never known.

There was only one way to take this wicked advantage from the rogue warlord: make sure that either nobody or *everybody* had these plans. Moonshadow stared at the inner workings of the doomsday musket. It was up to him to stop this nightmare in its tracks.

He rolled up the plans and eased them back into the bamboo tube. He slung the thong around his neck, then fed the tube carefully into his jacket, sliding it under both his night and mesh suits. The tube would keep the plans dry should he have to use the moat to escape. But was swimming out even an option now? His eyes flicked to the window. The glow behind those shutters was unmistakable. Moonshadow cursed silently. The sky was growing brighter still. Escaping via the moat was out of the question because very shortly the crescent moon would turn that shadowy moat into an archer's shooting gallery.

He stood tall on the chest, then bent his knees and made ready to launch himself upward for the second gap he had made in the ceiling.

In the distance, a conch shell horn sounded, the

type used to send signals in battle. Moonshadow's stomach churned and his heart sprinted into a flutter. What was happening? He hadn't set off any traps! He looked around frantically. Or had he? An alarm gong pealed from the castle's outer rectangle. Surely they were not under attack? Not at this hour!

Warning shouts came from somewhere far below in the castle grounds. He heard the urgent thrumming of feet on wooden stairs. *Guards, and lots of them.* They were inside the keep, on the next level down but rising fast. How, how had he been detected?

"They see him!" A fierce voice relayed the report in the corridor outside the treasure room. Moonshadow flinched hard. "The intruder's climbing down again!"

No he wasn't! Moonshadow tilted his head to one side, bewildered. The man outside was bellowing about something he hadn't done yet! Unless—

He blinked hard. Unless they had seen *another* intruder? A muffled *meow* came from the roof above him, echoing through the ceiling cavity. "Great timing," Moonshadow grumbled. *Now* the cat wanted to renew their friendship! There was another *meow*, a *thunk*, then a scraping sound as the roof tiles he had balanced collapsed into the hole he'd made. Moonshadow listened as the scraping turned to grinding, then stopped sharply. That infernal cat! It had tried to follow him into the ceiling, setting off the tile trap and blocking his escape hole! On the roof above, the animal began meowing, complaining because now it couldn't join him.

"Check the treasure room!" A guard's deep voice growled nearby. "There could be more!"

Moonshadow glanced at the door, then back up at the ceiling, momentarily confused. He was trapped! What to do? The keep's corridor floorboards pounded, the noise approaching fast. There were scuffing sounds, a sharp creak, then a tremble went through the treasure room's heavy sliding door. Moonshadow crouched low on the Chinese chest, holding his breath. The reinforced door flew open.

A dozen samurai stood outside, long swords already drawn. Moonshadow's hand slid into his leggings, probing for the high pocket where his *shuriken* and smoke bombs lay.

"There's one!" A powerful-looking swordsman pointed. "Take him!"

Roaring as one man, the twelve rushed in.

DETECTED

Moonshadow hurled a smoke bomb at the floor, then leaped for the opening above him.

With a low hissing, white smoke quickly filled the treasure room. The samurai plunged into it, stumbling over the low black cables, setting off chime traps as they ran for where they had last seen Moonshadow.

"Don't swing till you see him!" The swordsman leading them yelled. "Don't cut each other!"

The boards shook; the chime traps warbled.

Moonshadow dangled from the ceiling, swinging his legs. Below him, inside a white cloud, the guards collided with one another around the Chinese chest. Momentarily, they became a tight crush. Moonshadow swung himself hard and dropped, aiming his feet for the shoulders of the man nearest the door. The samurai snarled as Moonshadow landed on him, the impact sending him reeling backward.

Moonshadow sprang from the staggering samurai to the floor, bounded through the doorway, and twisted around fast. He quickly slid the reinforced door shut, snapping its wooden locking pin into place as the weight of twelve bodies shook it from the inside. Moonshadow ran along the corridor until he came to a window. Its shutters were open. He leapt up onto its sill, fished for his claws, and put them on, then hurriedly lowered himself onto the keep's wall outside. As he cleared the window and started down the side of the keep, the corridor he had just left echoed with the sounds of more shouting, running men. He descended faster.

The crescent moon was clearing the mountains now, splashing light over the tiles and beams of the castle's roofs. Shadows darting across the courtyard below and more frantic shouts from above suggested that an army of guards now converged on the keep and its treasure room.

Good. Moonshadow nodded. Let that diversion last as long as possible while he found his way out of here! He dropped smoothly to the rain roof, looking in all directions. He was now halfway back down the solitary tower. What was the fastest route out of this castle? He stared past the rain roof's chimney to the deserted archers' platform. That walkway would take him straight to the outer rectangle.

Hunching in shadow, Moonshadow stowed his claws, then listened and watched the walkway. No signs of life. The din of a panicky search continued to come from high up in the keep, but all was quiet in this little fold of the castle. He gave a sharp nod. Seize the advantage while it was there! Moonshadow stood up and scurried low across the rain roof.

Passing the chimney, he immediately sensed someone close behind him. Moonshadow spun about, but the foe was already springing from the chimney's tiny roof. Knuckles glanced off the side of his head. Moonshadow reeled backward, catching a glimpse of his attacker: a slender figure, dressed like him in a dark night suit, wearing a back-mounted sword. So there *was* another spy!

Moonshadow cartwheeled away to turn around in a strong upright stance, one hand on the grip of his sword. His mouth fell open. The rooftop was empty. Where did he go?

A knee slammed into his back from behind. He stumbled and groaned. This enemy could really jump! Moonshadow twisted about, brought his fists up, and used a scissor action to block a powerful incoming punch aimed at his throat. His agile enemy changed position with ease to sweep Moonshadow's feet out from underneath him. He crashed sideways to the tiles, forced to use his arms to break his fall. Seeing Moonshadow's guard down, his unknown foe pounced, dropping on top of him and revolving nimbly to elbow him hard between the eyes. The force of the blow jolted Moonshadow's head back. The rooftop around him instantly grew hazy. He tried to rise. His limbs were numb. He gasped, realizing that his attacker's cunning nerve-strike had paralyzed him. He was an easy kill now. Moonshadow willed his feet to move. They felt dead. The foe loomed over him, studying his night suit.

Crumpled against the tiles, Moonshadow waited for a sword's tip or edge to find him. Neither came. Instead of drawing a blade, his assailant crouched low and rammed one hand down the front of

Moonshadow's jacket; long, thin fingers probing for the bamboo and the plans. Moonshadow tried to move his feet again and this time felt them respond. He summoned up his strength and rolled, trapping his foe's legs, dragging the enemy to the rooftop beside him. Sustaining the roll, Moonshadow seized the stranger's wrist and twisted it fast, breaking the hold his opponent had on the leather thong around his neck.

Now Moonshadow further tangled the attacker's arms and legs with his own, gripping tightly as he rolled for the roof's edge. He sucked in an anxious breath. If he had rightly calculated the distance to the edge, momentum would help him fling his enemy from the roof. The other spy would have to abandon his attack to save himself from falling. If Moonshadow had figured the distance poorly, that edge would arrive too soon and they would both plunge over it, and anything could happen.

His sheathed sword dug into his back as he reached the final row of tiles. With a twist of his hips Moonshadow released his attacker, flicking him from the roof. Soundlessly the stranger fell. Moonshadow scrambled back from the edge, lungs heaving for air. He checked the leather thong, then patted the center of his chest. The bamboo tube was still in place. He carefully leaned from the roof, eyes hunting for signs of the other intruder on the face of the keep. His assailant hadn't tried to kill him when he could have, so Moonshadow hoped he had snatched a hold or found a landing point on the way down. But he saw nothing.

Moonshadow shuddered. His attacker had simply vanished. There was no hint of him clinging anywhere below the rain roof. No dangling rope, nor claw marks in the growing moonlight.

Had he overdone it, had the fall slain his opponent? Moonshadow's eyes probed lower. Nothing: no blood down the side of the building, no corpse at the bottom. He shook his head. Whoever his competitor was, his style was very different, but he was *good*. His distinctive moves looked so light and crisp, yet were deceptively powerful. Moonshadow clambered to his feet, glanced around warily, then focused on the walkway connected to the rain roof.

Someone else had found him, someone a little friendlier. Unable to help himself, Moonshadow grinned. The temple cat was crouched halfway along the walkway, head to the floor, apparently studying something trapped between its paws. His sense of relief started turning to elation, but years of training quickly cut in, warning him: *This was no time to relax.*

Moonshadow glanced over his shoulder. He had dealt with an unexpected complication, managing to survive it. But the real threat still lay ahead, the one he was always going to have to face: Silver Wolf's best guards, his finest castle samurai. And given the way the night had gone so far, who knew what else? Moonshadow licked dry lips.

He started forward onto the walkway. The cat looked up, glanced left and right, then leapt to its feet and ran to the edge. Moonshadow stopped as it jumped from sight into the darkness around the long archers' platform. He narrowed his eyes, peering further along the walkway.

Yes. There was a man, standing alone in shadow, blocking the path to the outer rectangle. A moment after seeing him, Moonshadow heard sounds from behind him.

Men, approaching stealthily.

Then the crescent moon burst above the castle's skyline and the whole suspended gallery was streaked with fingers of light.

Moonshadow slowly turned a circle. He was surrounded.

ENCIRCLED

Moonshadow eyed the lone figure on the walkway. If he overcame that one man, a path to the outer rectangle, and escape, was his.

Moonshadow advanced, darting quickly through the fingers of brightness, creeping watchfully through the bands of grey half-light.

On the walkway ahead, the man paced out of his shadow into a brighter spot. He pulled a short, *shinobi*-style sword from his belt and began tapping it, still in its scabbard, against one shoulder. Moonshadow studied him.

This one was balding and wiry. Clean-shaven. Hard eyes and a plain black robe. He was smiling, the manner of his walk deceptively casual. Moonshadow's mouth turned as dry as his lips. This fellow was very dangerous. There was skill in his aura, a cruel edge to his face.

The man looked Moonshadow in the eyes and bowed elegantly. Then his smile vanished. He started feeding his sword back into his belt.

Help me, Mantis, Moonshadow thought. What would *you* do if facing this opponent? He gave himself a subtle nod. Yes, that was it. *Use the enemy's confidence, his assurance that he's facing another* shinobi *and therefore predictable* shinobi *moves. Be unpredictable.*

Moonshadow stepped back into a patch of shadow and hunched low. Keeping his weapon hidden behind his body, he moved it from his back to his hip.

After tying it in place, he looked around.

Three men were sneaking up behind him. Two were uniformed samurai wearing household emblems: a tall fellow and his shorter sidekick. The third man's numerous tattoos said he was a gangster, no doubt from one of those big-town criminal gangs the Grey Light Order had, at times, infiltrated on behalf of the shogun.

The trio stopped moving. The tattooed one gestured to the lone figure blocking Moonshadow's path. It was not a polite gesture.

"Come on, Akira!" The gangster was playfully irritated. "Stop dragging it out. Get on with killing him; otherwise I *will* take the first turn." His voice dropped. "I still say it was rigged. We should have used *my* dice."

Moonshadow looked the complainer over. Many gangsters shaved their heads, but this one had long tangled hair, a messy beard, and a droopy moustache. His loudly patterned jacket bragged that he was proud to be an outlaw. Moonshadow was glancing at the man's forearm tattoos, red-green carps and dragons, when he realized that the gangster was holding a *shuriken* in each hand. Moonshadow set his jaw. This was no mere thug!

As he turned back to check on the man blocking his way, Moonshadow found the opponent creeping silently up to the edge of the shadow, one hand gliding to his sword's grip. He was dangerous all right. Moonshadow nodded. He was clearly *good*. He could move without a sound! But how well would he handle...*this?*

Lunging at his enemy but staying just inside the

shadow, Moonshadow drew his sword from the hip, duelist style.

The smallest fingers of his right hand pressed into the weapon's grip, tensing the blade as its tip was about to clear the mouth of the scabbard. As the draw accelerated, Moonshadow's left hand pulled and twisted the scabbard off the moving blade, keeping it under his belt, sliding it back around his waist. The combined, dynamic actions of each hand launched his sword tip at blinding speed.

In the moonlight, the explosive fast draw became a horizontal streak of silver, flashing momentarily from the cover of the shadow. The tip of Moonshadow's sword ambushed the lurking foe, who stood, still drawing his own weapon, at the edge of the better-lit ground. The man flinched and Moonshadow saw that his eyes were turned upward, as if he had been expecting a power cut from overhead. Aborting his own draw, the swordsman sprang back without a sound. Then he frowned, looked down, and clutched his right arm.

Moonshadow smiled to himself. Even the best could be undone by the power of surprise.

"Well you sure messed that up, Akira!" The gangster sniggered cheerfully. "So now it's Jiro's turn!"

Jiro raised one hand. Moonshadow dived forward into a shoulder roll. An instant later he heard the *clack clack* of two *shuriken* plowing into the walkway right where he had been.

There was no time to lose! Gaining his feet, he rushed the wounded Akira.

Akira parried Moonshadow's powerful diagonal cut and sliced back, narrowly missing Moonshadow's head. Next he aimed a sneaky sideways hack at Moonshadow's belly, but Moonshadow saw it coming and sprang into the air, raising both knees. Akira's blade glanced off the armor on Moonshadow's left leg, denting one panel. Moonshadow landed, regained his balance, and back-pedaled away. Akira rushed him with a series of wild horizontal swings, each one just missing its mark. Moonshadow dropped into a low crouch and lunged at his foe's closest ankle. Akira narrowly avoided the cut, jumping back out of sword range, chest heaving with exertion. Moonshadow shook his head. This man sure didn't fight like one with a deep cut to his arm! Then Moonshadow heard—and a second later felt—a *shuriken* whiz past his cheek. Akira dodged as it almost clipped him instead.

"Idiot!" Akira yelled. Frustrated at Jiro, he swung a hard rising cut at Moonshadow. Blocking it and seizing on his foe's broken balance, Moonshadow slipped past Akira and ran.

He dashed in a zigzag along the walkway. Dark figures pointed and shouted from the courtyard below. The crescent moon was higher overhead now, its light reaching further, thinning the shadows with each passing minute. Ahead, where the walkway ran out, he could discern a line of tiles, then another of huge stones.

It was the corner of the castle's outer rectangle that faced the town's sake brewery. And it was close! An arrow streaked up from the courtyard, whistling as it just missed his shoulder. He ran faster.

Four sets of feet pursued him, shaking the walkway. Moonshadow glanced back. Akira was at the rear now, which surprised Moonshadow. Perhaps he *had* cut the fellow badly. The gangster had fallen behind the two samurai. That was no surprise.

He looked ahead. The moonlight glinted on a cargo cable. It ran from the top of an iron mast planted in one of the corner's stone blocks. Moonshadow's mind raced. The cable ran to the sake brewery *across the moat*. A risky escape route, since it meant fixing himself to a predictable trajectory, but if he could somehow travel it fast... He glanced back at the pursuing samurai, their robes snapping as they ran.

The cable would have been the wrong way *in*, since it would always be watched by the nearest guards. But now, fleeing, his cover already lost, he realized that getting seen hardly mattered!

He thought of the samurai's uniforms. Yes, there *was* a way to do this.

Another arrow flashed up from the courtyard, burying itself in the platform's handrail beside him, its tail feathers trembling. Moonshadow reached the end of the walkway and jumped for the roof tiles. He bounded across the outer roof and landed on the tall block of stone from which the mast rose. Panting, Moonshadow looked back.

Akira had stopped before the end of the walk-way and was tying a tourniquet around his arm. The two samurai, as one might expect from professional warriors, were already scrambling with great deter-mination across the roof. The one nearest the stone was perhaps five seconds behind Moonshadow. The gangster was at their rear, weaving nervously over the roof with less than catlike agility.

Moonshadow took in the sake brewery end of the cable, then he spun back with his sword raised as the large samurai scrambled onto the stone block.

The samurai guard lunged at him. Moonshadow parried the attack, then turned the cutting edge of his sword quickly to hack at the foe's nearest wrist. But the guard had seen that trick before and he changed *his* grip fast, flicking his sword outward to block the slice.

Something blurred into the corner of Moonshadow's vision and instinctively he ducked. A *shuriken* hurtled just above his head, then another. He stood tall. The smaller samurai guard was struggling onto the block now. Moonshadow ignored him and charged the tall one.

Forcing the big samurai to block a fast series of slices with ever-changing angles, Moonshadow pressured the man into turning. Then relentlessly, cut by cut, he drove him backward at his colleague. Finally, Moonshadow gave a ferocious growl. He rushed the tall guard, locked swords with him, and pushed, sending the man crashing onto his partner.

Tangling in each other's limbs, the guards tumbled on the edge of the stone block. As they struggled to rise quickly without nicking one another, Moonshadow dropped to his knee and aimed a precision cut at the tallest samurai's thick cloth belt. His sword's tip sang true all the way to its target and the man's belt fell away, severed cleanly near its stomach knot.

Moonshadow stood up then jumped, aiming with

both feet for the samurai's belly. The man wheezed as Moonshadow landed on him, snatched the belt away, then pushed himself off hard. With a humiliated bellow the samurai angled a flailing cut up at Moonshadow, who blocked the rising sword with his leg armor, then scurried for the mast.

Enraged, the big samurai leapt up. His kimono swung open, revealing his carefully tied white loincloth. Like most traditional guards, he wore no mail or concealed armor. With a high-pitched grunt, he dropped his sword and frantically began tying the flaps of his clothing together.

Below the mast and its cable, Moonshadow sheathed the sword on his hip. He wound the stolen belt around one wrist, slung its length, double-folded, over the cable, caught the falling end, and wound that onto his free hand.

There was a sharp *crack*. Sparks flew from the mast beside his head. Moonshadow shuddered. Another *shuriken*! He looked around. The gangster was about to climb onto the stone block, and he obviously hadn't run out of throwing stars yet.

The tall samurai finished tying the front flaps of his kimono together. The guards exchanged nods and rushed Moonshadow, side by side, their swords swishing up into an overhead attack position.

Letting the cable take his weight, Moonshadow gripped the belt tightly and launched himself out over the moat. The cable creaked. Light as he was, he rapidly gained speed.

Halfway across and descending fast, a *shuriken* glanced off the armor of his right leg. He winced and cried out. The tip of one of its blades had punctured a joint in his armor, just missing the pockets, crammed with tools and clothing, above and below it.

He raised his leg and glanced down at it. There was a new pinprick hole in his legging, and he could feel a blood welt, right beneath it, on his thigh.

The outer bank of the moat flashed below. Moonshadow released the belt and dropped from the cable at the foot of the sake brewery. Just uphill, three huge wooden brewing barrels, each atop their own little tower, cast massive, dark shadows.

As he ran for their cover, a hail of arrows fell around him.

BLAME GAME

In the castle's finest landscape garden, Silver Wolf's two top guards, then Akira and Jiro, stood in a line, their heads bowed. Their master paced angrily before them, his face matching the dark clouds rolling in from the mountains.

Behind them, The Deathless sat on a granite boulder, dreamily brushing its dappled moss with his large fingers. He nodded slowly, feeling the strength of the rock beneath the softness of the moss.

He was unperturbed by Silver Wolf's lurking rage. Like this rock, he was weathered, hard, and patient, yet like its speckled covering, misleading with deceptive softness, at least so far. The Deathless grinned. His invincible edge would show itself soon. First, his experience told him, he should hold back, let his enemies themselves make his task simpler. Let this warlord fume, his minions fumble about.

The Deathless crumbled some moss between his thumb and finger, watching Silver Wolf grumble as he paced.

He had known there were two intruders in town, each young, powerful, and about to strike, for he had *felt* them. He'd watched one entering the castle and, if his impressions had been correct, had even sensed the second spy, further away, no doubt crossing the moat elsewhere to scale another wall. Their slightly different energies suggested they weren't of the same school, but each of them was *skilled*. The Deathless yawned beneath his hood. His master, Koga Danjo, before his...*untimely* death, had taught him far more than the greatest Old Country science. He had taught The Deathless to reason and to scheme about every situation. In the spirit world, no doubt Danjo regretted *that* now!

The two intruders The Deathless had sensed were probably among the best of a whole new generation of *shinobi*. By comparison, deathless or not, he was a scarred old war dog. He would let them compete, battle it out for the prize, then corner the exhausted winner, saving his strength in case they proved as strong as they felt. Yet he would prove superior: he the falcon, they the doves.

His eyes glided over his fellow hirelings. Along the way, these lesser men would be thinned out, for the pair they were up against clearly outclassed them.

Good! He alone would remain to make that final kill, and perhaps, as things grew more desperate for Silver Wolf, he could even raise his hefty fee a notch or two more.

The Deathless dropped his eyes to his seat of stone. He could make this work. But only if he remained as cool, as hidden, as that Ezo valley where he had been born. Double-faced, like this unbreakable rock and its misleading, passive moss.

"More rain in the next few days, then a storm, I would say." Silver Wolf took his eyes from the cloudy sky and continued pacing his landscape garden, hands clasped at his back. "But we have a greater problem than bad weather, don't we, gentlemen?"

On learning the plans had been taken, he had

exploded with rage, threatening to behead the unfortunate guard who had delivered the bad news. Once alone, Silver Wolf had hurled his writing kit against a wall. Along the way to his garden he'd barked at every maid, servant, and samurai he had encountered.

His fiery red fury had settled down now into brooding, white-hot malice. His every sarcastic word and chilling glance overflowed with it. But Silver Wolf knew self-control was vital if he was to salvage this disaster. As usual, he would have to do the thinking for his idiot men. He took a steadying breath. This peaceful garden always helped clear his mind. It was where he came to find solutions when things went wrong. As they had last night, and *badly*.

He crossed a small wooden bridge over the garden's spring-fed stream, stopping at a stone lantern under a maple tree. Muttering, Silver Wolf shook his head and walked on. Rounding a miniature "sea" of raked sand, he strode back to the group of waiting, uneasy men.

The warlord eyed his hirelings coldly as he approached, making no effort to hide his contempt for them. He was tempted to slay at least one for last night's miserable effort, but then he would never get his money's worth out of whomever he chose to kill. Besides, their job wasn't done yet, and he still needed them all. With his guidance, they might yet redeem themselves. *If not...*

"Anyway... finish your report!" the warlord grunted at Akira.

The spy cleared his throat. "Before sunrise, I went with Jiro and your men to the inn your informer spoke of. The innkeeper there agreed he'd just had such a customer: a messenger boy, the right age and build, and what's more, a stranger to the town. But that boy vanished last night. Nobody near the inn has seen him since."

Silver Wolf was thoughtful. "Akira, though you failed last night, it was you who dueled our intruder before his escape on the cable. As your wound proves, *you* were closest to the action. So, what else can you tell me?"

"Forget last night, Lord, he won't escape us again!" Jiro butted in. "My gangsters now watch every exit from town, with orders to stop and search any young male of slight build! A bit more time, that's all we need. He'll be found."

"Which your heads won't be, if he gets away." Silver Wolf stared each of them down, ending with Jiro. "Or if you speak again without first being spoken to."

Jiro dropped to one knee and lowered his head.

Akira gave a weary sigh. "There were two of them, Lord, which added to the confusion last night."

"Who was the other?" Silver Wolf folded his arms. "An accomplice to the one you fought?"

"I don't think so, Lord. His kind, like me, prefer to work alone." Akira gave Jiro a cold sideways glance. "Professionals find the presence of others a hindrance. No, I would say that second intruder was a rival, a rival of equal skill to the one who took your plans." He went to add something, then stopped himself.

The warlord gestured impatiently. "What else? Come on, out with it, man!"

"I was the one who saw the other intruder on the wall of the keep, Lord. I would say from the figure's light movements and peculiar agility that it was a girl."

"Maybe you should have fought *her*," Jiro mumbled. "Man with the big reputation."

Akira rounded on him, hand moving to his sword. "Lucky I'm still alive to fight anyone for our Lord! Half your *shuriken* flew nearer *me* than *him*!"

Jiro's hand flashed into his jacket. He shuffled one step back. "Oh, now it's all *my* fault! Who demanded first try at the enemy? Who cheated and won the dice roll? Who—"

"Silence!" Silver Wolf snapped. "Unhand your weapons! *I* will decide where blame is laid and who shall die for it!" He raised one eyebrow. This gangster scum had made a good point, though. Who had failed him most the night before? He stared at each of his samurai, then the hirelings, leaving The Deathless till last.

It had been agreed that The Deathless be held in reserve, the others forming the first wave against any intruder. But their overnight visitor had proved too strong for that first wave. Silver Wolf narrowed his eyes. Surely The Deathless must have been watching? Why didn't he simply jump in and deal with that intruder, who was so obviously a worthy match for him?

Silver Wolf watched the tall assassin flicking moss. Reason cooled his anger. He wanted to demand answers, but what if he made an enemy of the killer? After all, The Deathless was a dangerous living legend, and since he was immune to blades, not even a warlord could threaten him with death. Silver Wolf hid a sly smile. Of course, his magic probably did not extend to guns. He might have to consider that option, if his most expensive hireling didn't do *something*. And soon.

The Deathless looked up and appeared to read

Silver Wolf's mind. His soulless eyes locked on his master's face.

"Have no concern, my Lord," he said slowly. "The matter isn't settled yet. I sense our thief is still in town. Be assured: I will conduct my own search, my way, and pounce when the time is exactly right. If your other...*employees* here do not redeem their failure first, then it is I who in time will recover your plans. *And* this boy spy's head."

Silver Wolf met the killer's unblinking gaze. A bold promise! He would have mocked anyone else making it, or warned them to make good on their word or die, just as he had with Jiro. The warlord drew a slow breath. But no. *Not with this man.*

Instead, he thought aloud. "So! There's another spy. And it's a girl?"

"I am quite sure of it, Lord." Akira bowed. "A girl, and his rival."

"She too," The Deathless said, crumbling moss between his fingers, "is still here."

"Sir." The tallest samurai turned. "No disrespect, but how can you know that?"

The Deathless pointed at Akira then back to himself. "All *shinobi* are taught to detect each other. As Akira-San has shown, even when disguised, the subtle moves of one's body betray information to a trained eye. As we hone our craft, some of us even learn to sense each other's presence *directly*. But that's an imperfect science, and few reach the level where their *impressions* are consistently accurate." He paused. "I have."

"What matters is that they are both still here." Silver Wolf was heartened by the news. "I see the way ahead! We'll make this rival work for us, then kill the pair of them."

Jiro sprang to his feet. "Great idea, my Lord!" His nose creased. "But how?"

"All of you, forget trying to find the boy. He's obviously well hidden now in town, no doubt waiting for the right chance to bolt. Therefore, make no loud house-to-house searches for him. I will have that particular corner swept by a more subtle broom."

"Then what should *we* do, Lord?" Akira rubbed the bandage on his arm.

"Concentrate on finding this girl. She must appear in *some* guise by daylight. You, Akira: brief the others on her build and that distinctive agility. Let The Deathless here use his sensing powers! All of you: disguise yourselves. Comb the streets. Try to recognize her walk or manner."

Jiro looked confused. "And then?" Akira rolled his eyes.

"Follow her, you fool! She is this boy's rival, yes? Let her lead us to him *and* my plans. And when you get another chance, your second try at one or both of them, take no risks!" He pointed sternly at his best guards. "Use our horses and capture chains trick to bring them down! Those unusual tactics should surprise even *shinobi*!" The two samurai bowed quickly. Silver Wolf gave a low hiss. "But know this, each of you. My patience now lies stretched, like rice paper about to tear. Fail me again…" he had to stop himself. Rage was swelling inside him once more.

The Deathless cracked his knuckles. The tall samurai closed his eyes. Akira stood stony-faced, unblinking. Jiro glanced back at the hooded assassin and swallowed hard.

Silver Wolf turned away. "Now get out of my sight!"

BRAVADO AND
BAD TIMING

Groundspider, in his favorite guise—the gregarious silk merchant—pounded his way along a lonely coastal strip of the Tokaido. He had cleared the Hakone Barrier without incident, though he'd been sorely tempted to duel one of the cocky samurai there who had snapped at him when he'd reached for his papers.

The most bandit-plagued part of the Hakone forest and the tranquil lake district below it were also behind him now, and Groundspider was starting to believe that this phase of his mission was actually *meant* to run smoothly.

"Just goes to prove," he mumbled to himself, "how much the gods love me."

He looked ahead from under the brim of his sun hat and knew at once that he had spoken too soon. A steely-eyed inspector, one of the so-called public service samurai who assisted magistrates and other court officials, was striding toward him.

Inspectors were roving assessors, ever watchful for threats to public order, and though they rarely took direct action themselves, they were notorious for reporting suspicious or even just unfamiliar faces to the nearest authorities. Groundspider maintained the simpering grin and oafish gait of his merchant character.

He felt the inspector's eyes lock onto him. Just a few paces more, Groundspider thought, and we'll pass each other by, and it will all be over. He took care not to look too sharp, too aware, lest the inspector decide that something about his manner and his eyes did not align. It was crucial that *nothing* captured the man's attention. As the two travelers passed closely, Groundspider slowed and politely bowed without stopping. The inspector nodded, looked him up and down with a frown, and kept walking.

Groundspider let out a long sigh. Good! That wrinkle in his mission plan could so easily have become a tear. He relaxed a little, then glanced up again at the highway ahead. More trouble! In fact, he sensed, *worse* trouble. The muscles of his abdomen tightened.

A stocky ronin samurai stood in the path, hands on his hips, eyeing Groundspider. The man wore a single sword, belted and tied in the manner of a seasoned duelist. He was a hand-span or two shorter than Groundspider, but his aura suggested that he was actually far more vigorous than he looked. The samurai seemed relaxed, confident too, and the light in his eyes warned of a hidden purpose. Groundspider continued to furtively study the fellow as he approached him. Not one scar on his face, which was never a good sign.

"Oi!" The man pointed at Groundspider. "Trader! There's some bad territory between here and the next town. A man with a fine jacket like *that* shouldn't be without a bodyguard in these parts. Lucky for you, I'm for hire."

"Sorry," Groundspider said in his best Nagasaki accent, "but I have no money with which to pay you, only silk samples…all small and worthless in themselves!" He awkwardly hefted his large traveling pack from his shoulder and plunged a hand inside it, fingertips seeking the hilt of his concealed sword. "Want to see some fine white silk?"

"No." The ronin took a step forward, hands gliding to his own sword. "But you can pay me with that jacket."

"Must I?" Groundspider feigned clumsiness with the handling of his pack even as his hand closed around the grip of his weapon. He readied himself to draw and strike without warning. His plan was simple: wound the fool, scare him witless, then walk on briskly. His training and experience made him hesitate. This was the most desolate strip of the whole highway, with not a soul in sight behind the ronin, but he was still about to break rules, take a crazy chance, and indulge himself in a way that would have Eagle snapping and Mantis lecturing him…if they were here! Groundspider hid the start of a grin. But they weren't here, were they? And this ronin was just too annoying to ignore. He was going to do it. He'd give this thug his first scar, a nice clean one on his cheek, to remind him always of his mistake. A mere second or two later, his *shinobi* sword would be repacked, with only the shaken ronin the wiser. Yes. Why not? He rarely got to have any fun!

"You know," Groundspider said, "I'd rather *not* make that deal."

"*I insist*," the ronin snarled, slowly drawing his sword. Since he took his time, he'd clearly assumed that he was dealing with an unarmed, easy target.

Groundspider's sword flashed from the pack, its tip flying for the ronin's cheek. Taken by surprise, the ronin flinched to one side, then released his half-drawn sword and clutched the side of his head with both hands, letting out a howl of pain.

Groundspider grinned. Then a stern voice made him freeze.

"What outrage is this? An unauthorized duel?" Sandals crunched the grit of the road behind him as Groundspider quickly repacked his sword.

"You, merchant, turn! Face me." The inspector drew his own weapon.

THE HUNTED

At the foot of the sake brewery's hill lay the town's poorest street.

It stood on low ground that often flooded. Half its homes and businesses had been abandoned, and those still occupied were in urgent need of repair. The whole street showed signs of recent water damage from heavy spring rains.

Its smallest building, a badly run-down stable, stood rotting near the edge of town, a stone's throw from the bright red shrine that welcomed travelers entering Fushimi.

Other than rats, the near-ruined stable had only two occupants now. An ancient, retired packhorse, and Moonshadow.

Moonshadow lay in a wide, deep bed of half-rotten rice straw, one hand on the plans around his neck, his hood off but night suit and leg armor still in place. He lapsed in and out of sleep. The old, weary-looking grey horse stood chewing, watching him.

Beside the stable's door, half planks had rotted away, creating a thin window just wide enough for the horse to use. Every so often, growing bored with watching the boy in the straw, the horse would swing around, poke his head outside, and stare off down the street, chewing contentedly. Now the animal gave a loud snort. Moonshadow sat up. He tried again to shrug off the urge to sleep. Under his armor, his legs were covered in bruises and blood-welts. His back, left shoulder, and every limb ached. Last night had taken far more energy than expected. Moonshadow rubbed his eyes and listened to the traffic passing on the street outside. The horse returned his sleepy stare, then turned and put its head out through the window.

Moonshadow briefly considered sight-joining with the horse and using the animal as a lookout, since it was so intent on watching the street anyway.

But quickly he realized that his energy was too depleted for a sight-joining, even the basic kind.

He recalled, as Nanashi, once overdoing it with the beast sight and the humiliation it had cost him. When he'd first made progress with the science, Eagle had warned him to pace himself and rest up between experiments, lest exhaustion ambush him. Swept along by the heady joy of mastering something new, he had ignored the warning. Three days in a row he'd linked himself to different creatures: a dog, then a pigeon, and finally, at sunset on the third day, a bat.

When Nanashi had failed to appear for the evening meal, Groundspider had been sent to search for him. Finding him under a tree in a death-like sleep, the big oaf had been unable to resist temptation. With a stick of charcoal, Groundspider had written "turnip skull" and "maker of foul gas" on Nanashi's forehead before carrying him to the dinner table. Nanashi had woken to wry smiles and crafty gleams in almost everyone's eyes. Badger alone had kept a straight face. But that was Badger.

At bedtime, Heron, smiling behind her hand, had held out a wet cloth and told him—in a tone of playful guilt—what had happened.

He had taken his revenge on Groundspider a

month later, furtively smearing the ravenous one's rice bowl with an oil that brought on hours of diarrhea.

Moonshadow closed his eyes, wishing he were home.

No, he could risk no sight-joining today. It was too soon, and more than a brotherly prank would await him if his enemies found him in a deep sleep. He should rouse himself and keep watch the hard way for a while. This was no place to be ambushed in. Escape might not be easy.

The stable had only one door. Like the horse's spy-hole, it faced the street. The only way in or out. Moonshadow scratched his cheek thoughtfully. If he had to leave fast, it would be no use counting on that excuse of a window. The horse might be using it at the time. The boards around it were rotten, which was also a hazard. He'd staggered in here, desperate to rest, but now regretted his choice of hideout: it was never a good tactic to box oneself in.

He'd assailed the castle on his first day in Fushimi, and the out-of-town rendezvous was scheduled for tomorrow, not today. He couldn't imagine, in this condition, waiting in some forest near the meeting place, at the mercy of rain and overnight cold. He had been told there were chalk caves in the area, but what if he couldn't find one?

Perhaps he *should* have held off until the second night before striking.

Moonshadow wondered about the other spy who had attacked him just before he'd encountered the guards. How exactly had he vanished after being flipped from the roof? And to where? Moonshadow's battle with castle security must have been a fine diversion, enabling the spy's smooth escape. He found himself smiling. Whoever that spy was, his skills were intriguing. His sheer energy and slight build suggested youth. He nodded. So he *wasn't* the only young *shinobi* in the field. Was *that* agent's world as solitary as his, or did he, like some adult spies, also have a daytime identity, a life that included unsuspecting friends? Moonshadow sighed. He'd like such a life.

He rotated his shoulder. It clicked painfully. He could not afford to be cornered while so utterly spent. If he were forced to fight now, a mere castle samurai would probably be able to wound him. He needed a full day's rest for his strength to return. This stable's layout was such a problem. It left him blind and vulnerable. His pursuers could approach the building, unseen, at any time. He stared at the ragged wooden door. If that duelist in the black robe, that Akira, burst through it while he lay in some fitful sleep...a desperate fight, no doubt to the death, would follow.

Moonshadow thought of his duel with Akira on the suspended walkway, how Mantis's advice had guided him to snatch the advantage. He had wounded the man in black, but how would he feel today, if instead he had killed him outright with that cut?

He remembered Mantis telling him a dueling anecdote, one that he often remembered when he looked into his teacher's solemn eyes. Nanashi, as he was then, had—somewhat thoughtlessly—raised Brother Eagle's disclosure that Mantis had been a professional duelist, as Eagle had said, "in the wildness of his youth."

Mantis had almost scowled at the obvious hero worship in his student's eyes. After thinking awhile, he had spoken of once wandering into a town where, as it turned out, a great sword contest was being held—one offering the winner a large cash prize.

"On the dusty street outside the training hall sponsoring the event," Mantis said, "I was accosted by a tall, skinny samurai who carried two swords, and also wore a curious, colorful head-binding, so all that showed were his eyes. He

told me my single-sword school was inferior, the very spit of cockroaches, as I recall. At first, I just insulted him back. 'Go hit your head,' I snarled, 'on a wet piece of tofu, and die!' "

The impatient young Nanashi was barely able to contain his enthusiasm. "But you *did* fight him, right there and then, for the insult, huh?"

"I considered it, sure, because back then I was as hot-headed as you are now," Mantis said ruefully, "but I chose to wait until the official matches later that day. I wanted that prize money, you see." He groaned mildly. "My pride, like my honor, had a price in those days. Anyway, the rules stated that the contestants had to duel until one surrendered or blood was drawn. But this lanky rooster, just as we were about to fight each other, suddenly demanded a death match, which could only be held with the consent of both swordsmen. Since he went on insulting me, I agreed. Of course, the bloodthirsty crowd who was watching loved it, and was roused to bet wildly on the outcome. I told my antagonist to take off his head wrap and reveal himself, but instead he just shouted a final taunt, saying that he showed his face only to real men." Mantis sighed. "That did it. I was furious. We fought. He was good, surprisingly good. But I was better. I killed him."

"Aw, he asked for it!" Nanashi folded his arms with a lofty sneer.

Mantis closed his eyes before saying more. "When he fell, I stepped back, and the competition's doctors removed his head-wrap. The crowd gasped. He was not much older than you are now. Freakishly tall, but in truth, just a silly boy."

"But he could really handle a sword, two in fact!" Nanashi protested. "Doesn't that make it fair?"

"A thing can be fair," Mantis said quietly, "yet still be wrong."

He then fixed Nanashi with a disturbing, unfamiliar stare. "I see them, you know, some nights, when I dream... all the men I've killed. I see that mouthy kid too; he's with them. They all wait for me... in a tavern, in the land of the dead."

"Do they hate you?" Nanashi had quickly asked. "Do they want vengeance?"

"No." Mantis had flashed a strange smile. "They hold up their sake cups and say: 'Come on, drink with us, there are no hard feelings. We were all just young fools!' That is my recurring dream, but in truth, I think it is actually my heart's constant prayer—forgiveness."

Mantis's face and words faded, and Moonshadow stared at the door. No! He couldn't be trapped in here. The pressure of being cornered would almost certainly guarantee that someone would die, and it seemed his teacher's example had been etched into his soul.

He crawled to the largest knothole in the door and began watching the street through it with one eye. Later, he would dig up the sack he had already buried at the back of the stable. In it lay the trappings of his next identity: the jacket, belt, and wadded pants of a young merchant's clerk. He even had an abacus. Wrung out as he was, Moonshadow smiled. The clothes-drying poles and laundries of Fushimi had served him well. Tomorrow, dressed as a clerk, he would proceed to the rendezvous point, where Grey Light Order agents would meet him. Whoever turned up would bring his last disguise, the one that would see him back to Edo. To safety, and to home.

A family of peasant farmers carrying baskets of vegetables drifted by. Farther along the street, a wandering priest in a huge woven hat was trying to sell good luck charms to a pair of excitable teenage girls. Moonshadow looked the other way and gasped. A familiar, big-boned man carrying a long staff waddled toward the stable. Private Investigator Katsu! Still dressed as a town businessman, the snoop was going house to house alone, quietly checking the whole derelict street.

As Moonshadow watched, Katsu flushed out a homeless outcast, a ragged older man wearing a faded red sash. Moonshadow felt sad for the frail-looking peasant who bowed low to Katsu and scurried away between the buildings. The red sash, which he could never take off, meant he had been convicted of a serious crime, most likely a robbery. That sash was an order to anyone he met, an order to ignore him and offer no food, work, or shelter. It was a *living* death sentence. Moonshadow hung his head with a grim smile. At least that would never happen to him. Spies were *always* executed, the good old-fashioned way.

"Hello, old horse!" Moonshadow watched in horror as Katsu strolled up to the stable door.

CORNERED

Moonshadow leapt to his feet. He took a deep breath, summoning up his resolve, pooling all his remaining strength. Then he vaulted up into a corner of the stable facing the street. On the opposite side of the door to the horse's window, where the leaky ceiling met the rotting wall, he gripped the rafters and splayed out like a great spider.

The door creaked open. Katsu peered around the doorframe first before stepping inside. He amiably patted the horse's flank, his eyes sweeping around the stable. The horse pulled its head inside and, with a friendly sputter, turned to watch the visitor.

Moonshadow, already struggling to maintain his grip, looked down on Katsu from behind.

Unlike a *shinobi*, this man did not begin searching a room by looking high and turning in a circle. Detective or not, he was like most people: he barely looked up at all. Moonshadow grinned. This fellow was not accustomed to dealing with spy-kind.

School time, Katsu!

Then his neck abruptly went weak. His last two sight-joinings, the carp and the cat, falling so close together, had already pushed him too far. Suddenly Moonshadow could feel his vital *ki* energy, his life force, ebbing away. Hurry up, Detective, he thought tersely. Either give up and go, or look up and make me kill you. Either way, do it fast, please, before I faint and land at your feet.

Katsu took one end of his staff in both hands and started carefully probing the deep layer of scattered rice straw. Moonshadow's eyelids flickered. A dark wave rolled over him. He forced his eyes wide open. His left shoulder was throbbing hard now.

During every year of his training, he had worked with a bean-shaped, rice-straw dummy *exactly* matching his own weight at the time. He had lifted it fifty times a day and now could hold his body against most ceilings for over an hour.

But not this morning. A chill went through Moonshadow as he realized it. In about thirty seconds, whether clinging up here or lying down there, he was going to black out.

Snowhawk crouched low in the narrow alley across the road from the stable.

The big man swung the stable door shut with his staff as he exited. A tired-looking old horse poked its head out through a gap in the wall and the fellow turned around and patted its muzzle, saying goodbye.

She stayed in shadow, watching as the snoop stretched before plodding off down the street. It seemed his search of Fushimi's poor district was finished. If so, there was a mystery here. This searcher had obviously left empty-handed, yet Snowhawk could sense the boy spy in that stable. Surely *he* was the one being hunted. So what was going on here?

Crossing the street, she furtively checked the big-boned figure ambling into the distance. Disguised now as a young weaver's apprentice in a drab hemp work kimono—a stolen one, of course—Snowhawk knew she could walk the streets unnoticed, at least by ordinary citizens. It was Silver Wolf's specialists, professionals like herself, that she had to be wary of. They too altered their appearance all the time. Her eyes flicked around. That hunchbacked farmer, one or all of those fit young brewery workers, *anyone* could be a *shinobi* in the service of Fushimi's lord. She stopped in front of the stable door. But her exceptional senses told her that only one like herself was nearby right now. *Him.*

He was in there. She could feel it: a clear, strong impression. If only she could avoid combat with him … get close enough to use her *special* talent. This boy was good—in fact, he was brilliant. Snowhawk smiled. But so were the last three warriors she had used her unique gift on. Before this day ended, those plans would be hers after all.

As she gripped the ragged door, a dull *whump* came from the other side of it. She knew that sound; she had made it herself more than once. A body landing in straw. Snowhawk frowned. It hadn't sounded like a very controlled landing, though. Too loud.

Maybe he was injured. Not too badly, she hoped! Snowhawk bit her lip. Why did she care? This was confusing. She would take the plans from him. She had to. But also, undeniably, she wanted to see him again. She had so many questions. Snowhawk sighed. Talking to him might be an unwise, even crazy idea, but a longing burned inside her. She wanted a friend. A friend that might actually understand her situation—its emptiness, its fear.

Why, what was the point? *This* hadn't happened to her before!

Snowhawk opened the creaky door slowly. There he was, stretched out in the straw, his face slightly ashen. Was he dying or critically exhausted? She slipped into the stable and closed the door. He was in the deep sleep of one utterly spent. She leaned over him. Potential friend or relentless enemy? Either way, here was her best chance yet to study him closely. Whichever path the future took, such knowledge would be useful. So what could she read in his appearance?

The boy had a lush head of long, black hair, its shine suggesting he was well fed and made to groom regularly. He had a long face, free of scars so far. Was that a sign of limited experience in the field? His features lacked the roundness of a farmer's face. Instead he had a pointy chin and high cheekbones. She studied his straight nose and thin lips. Snowhawk frowned. That face was almost aristocratic. Was he an orphan, like her? If so, there was no telling where he had originally come from. He appeared slightly taller than most boys his age, naturally lean and flexible looking, too. Perhaps also a hint of general good health and breeding in his bloodline? His fingers were long, almost delicate, but those hands still looked very strong. The shape of his limbs implied lots of dense muscle that could only have come from an upbringing full of hard training. Her eyes glided over his night suit to the leg armor.

He sat up sharply, one hand moving for his sword. Snowhawk leapt back into a defensive posture. His eyes focused, then darted up and down as he studied her build and the crisp lines of her stance. Recognition flickered in his face.

"The ambush on the rain roof!" he whispered. "It was you!"

Which way would this go? He still hadn't drawn his weapon. She watched his eyes carefully. At first they were hard with alarm and wariness. Then she saw a strong flare of curiosity in them. The advantage was hers again: if he too was curious, she'd be able to get close. Which meant victory!

She held up her hands and smiled. "Don't kill me just yet. First let me thank you properly for what you did back on the road."

His probing eyes suddenly narrowed suspiciously. "You didn't really need my help with those bandits."

"Maybe not, but what you did was both brave and kind. Thank you." Snowhawk bowed, keeping her gaze on him.

"Thank *you*," he said coolly, "for not killing me last night."

Snowhawk raised her eyebrows and could not resist a smirk. "You're welcome."

"Why didn't you kill me then?" The boy shook his head. "You had the upper hand, yet chose not to use your sword. If you had, I'd be dead now and you'd have the plans. So tell me...*why?*"

She shrugged. "I don't know." But Snowhawk knew the curiosity burning in her own eyes gave a more honest answer. She caught herself at it: wondering about him, about his life, whom he served. If he, like her, would appreciate having just one real friend?

The mission! She had to take herself in hand and put the mission first. After all, her life depended on its success. She dropped to her knees at the edge of the straw. He flinched, but let her stay there. Good! Despite any questions she might have, there was a job to do, an important, urgent job. Right now, only he stood in the way of its completion.

"Can there be a truce between us?" he asked hopefully with a cautious grin.

"On one condition." She flashed her loveliest smile and saw it work on him. "That you tell me your name. I'll give you mine too, of course. Then we can be"— Snowhawk creased her nose playfully—"friends."

The boy leaned forward. She sensed him weighing carefully what he would say next. "My name is Nanashi."

With an effort, Snowhawk kept her face passive. *Nanashi?* Wasn't that an Edo dialect word for *nameless?* She crept forward softly. "Pleased to meet you. I am Yuki."

Snowhawk was certain he had lied, just as she had. They had been trained to. Why hadn't he bothered to give a more convincing name? No matter. He was sufficiently off-guard. It was time to get on with the task. She stole closer, looking deep into his eyes.

"You are weary," she whispered. "Let me help you up." As he took her outstretched hand, she drew a soft breath and unleashed her most dangerous skill at him. Her stomach turned hot and her heart pounded. Snowhawk felt a familiar invisible energy surge from her eyes to his. But would he be that rare exception who was immune to it? The boy's eyelids quickly sagged. No, he was susceptible, just like the others! She released another dose at him. His eyes almost closed and his hand relaxed, falling from hers. Part of her didn't want to go on, but she doggedly fired a third silent, powerful bolt.

Three had always been enough. The heat in Snowhawk's stomach faded. Her heart slowed.

Now the boy's eyes glazed over. He fell back into the straw with a soft *whump*, eyes rolling back in his head just before their lids came down. She nodded. It was done.

He was in the grip of *shinobi* hypnosis now, hers to command or kill. She gave a weak, guilty smile. *Or to spare.*

Snowhawk darted forward and hovered over him. She patted his chest until she felt the bamboo tube. Slipping the thong from around his neck, she pulled the tube from his jacket. Holding it up, she unstopped the end and took out the plans. A quick scan convinced her they were real. Snowhawk packed them away again, then slipped the thong around her own neck. She glanced down at the boy. He began to snore.

"This, *Nanashi*, is not a sleep you can shake off," she told her victim. "You will now sleep all day, all night. If *they* don't find you first, you should wake feeling quite rested."

She stood tall, looked down on him, and shook her head.

"What a waste," Snowhawk muttered. "Now *you'll* be killed for failure."

TO ROB A THIEF

The next day it began to rain just after dawn. The downpour woke Moonshadow.

He sat up and looked around. The horse was staring at him, its ears twitching. He rose, feeling surprisingly refreshed as he dug up the sack. Changing clothes over his thin wire mesh suit, Moonshadow quickly transformed into a young merchant's clerk, complete with an abacus dangling from his belt.

He glanced at the stable door and sighed with relief. The gods had to be with him; he'd managed to rest and regain his strength here, without being discovered after all! His eyes glided back to his sword.

Wait! He had reached for that while in here. When? Why? Moonshadow flinched, swamped by a sudden flood of returning memories.

He *had* been discovered in here! By *her*. Something had dulled his wits but yesterday was coming back to him now. His eyes flared wide. His hand slapped against his chest, palm probing for the bamboo tube beneath the wire under-suit. No tube, no thong, nothing! The plans were gone. "Yu-ki!" he snarled.

Moonshadow screwed his eyes shut and shook his head hard with a long, frustrated hiss. How could he have been so reckless? He'd let her get close, far too close. He ground his teeth. What had she done to him? He remembered going through the facade of polite introductions, doubting the name she had given him, and her offer to help him up...

After that, his recall was a fog. What had happened next? Had he seen her open the door and go, or just dreamed it? From the moment he had taken her hand, things were hazy.

"Groundspider is right!" He cuffed at his own head. "Gullible! Stupidly gullible!" Moonshadow gnashed his teeth, confused and miserable, angry with "Yuki" and with himself. Her sly tricks had swiped victory from his hands, or rather, from around his neck.

This, his first real mission, meant everything, and he was *desperate* not to fail. But now, because of her—

He hastily stowed his spying tools in his backpack, then tied the pack and slung it beside another brand-new item he had stolen: a reed-matting bedroll that hid his sword. He peered outside through the horse's spy-hole. The rain had driven most people indoors, but now he couldn't afford to stay sensibly dry. Moonshadow scowled. He had to find *her* and get those plans back, and fast. He closed his eyes, reaching out with his feelings, trying to sense *shinobi* energy. He felt *something*, but detecting other spies by impression was difficult, and had never been one of his strengths. Still, an instinct told him that it was her he felt, and nearby. Placing confidence in that idea was risky. It meant relying on an instinct not much better than guesswork. But it was a thread of hope he gratefully snatched for. Moonshadow blew air between his lips. On this mission, he'd already been forced to take gambles. Now this *big* one was required. He threw open the stable door. No time to lose: even if he was right and she was still close by, she wouldn't tarry long in Fushimi, having snatched the objective from him. It would be too much to hope that his second chance would last more than a day.

Moonshadow walked the streets in the steady spring rain, watchful but grumbling under his breath.

Groundspider must never learn of this. He scowled. Tricked...robbed...by a *girl* spy? His desperate gaze swept porches, alleys, distant figures shuffling under paper umbrellas. No sign of her yet. She was probably waiting for a break in the weather, so that if she was pursued, a muddy bog of a road wouldn't slow her down or limit her fighting tricks. A smart tactic, he begrudgingly noted. Was she laughing at him right now, as she sat somewhere nice and dry, drinking tea and gloating over *his* plans? He let fly with a curse. Well he was going to have the last laugh *and* complete his mission.

Moonshadow glanced up, an evil smile twisting his lips. When the sky cleared and he found this *Yuki*, he'd make her pay all right, by taking back his plans in broad daylight and more! Moonshadow's hands curled into fists. He wasn't being cruel; it was only fair. Whatever she had done to him hadn't involved pressure points or potions, so had to be an Old Country science. His eyes gleamed. Two could play at that game. He, Moonshadow of the Grey Light, would give her a messy lesson in special powers she would never forget! He'd try to make a whole flock of pigeons circle over her, doing what pigeons did best...all over shrines and temples.

Hah! Like those peasant girls he had seen on the journey, caught in sudden rain, Yuki would run, squealing and distracted, so worried about her ruined hair and clothes she'd be easy prey for his surprise tackle.

Moonshadow stopped, wet and frustrated. No trace of her. His trawling of the muddy streets had taken him in great circles, and now he was back where he had started. The poor street and its stable lay behind him.

Nearby stood the red shrine on the edge of town. There the main road widened as it curved its way out of Fushimi. Just over the next range of hills the road split, one fork turning north for the Tokaido, the other heading west to Kyoto.

An idea came to him, inspired by his plan of revenge-by-pigeon. He hurried to the shrine, dodging muddy potholes in the road. The shrine's well kept red buildings and massive wooden gate loomed in his path. Moonshadow's eyes flicked to the property next door, a rich merchant's house.

Between the merchant's house and the busy main road was a walled garden. Moonshadow smiled secretively. There he could hide and wait for a bird to land. A bird that could fly, rain or no rain, all over town until it chanced upon *her*. He sighed, his shoulders falling. Maybe not a plan assured of success, but the best he could think of for now. After making certain that no one was watching, Moonshadow leapt onto the high stone wall, then climbed down into the leafy garden.

He listened to the sound of the rain hissing in the garden's single large pond. No birds drinking from it now, but they would be along once the rain eased. He frowned. Where could she be hiding? He was still sensing *shinobi* energy, and it felt a little stronger now, so she wasn't far away. The rain began to ease. Every tree, vine, and shrub dripped noisily. He turned a circle slowly, inspecting the garden.

Four stone walls enclosed it. Around the pond, small shrubs had been sculpted into dramatic shapes. The wall that separated the garden from the merchant's house was broken by a bamboo gate. On each side of the gate hung a thick curtain of vines. Moonshadow nestled himself into them, pressing his back against the stone wall. Now he could watch the pond from hiding.

As the rain settled down to a misting drizzle, the first bird arrived. A fat pigeon, it drank greedily, bathed, then began waddling around the pond, pecking for worms the rain had brought to the surface. Moonshadow prepared to sight-join with the pigeon. This would be easy; he had linked to just this type of bird once before.

A black-and-white blur leapt silently from the outer wall to the ground. Moonshadow's head turned sharply at the movement, then he smiled. The oddball temple cat! Either unaware of Moonshadow or ignoring him, the cat hunched low and commenced stalking the pigeon. Its tail swished as it crept along, belly almost dragging on the wet ground.

Voices drifted from beyond the wall. The cat turned its head toward the sounds. The pigeon, detecting movement at its back, made a quick airborne escape. Moonshadow realized that with the rain slowing, the road would quickly grow busy again. People entering and leaving Fushimi would hurry about their business before more showers struck. His eyes lit up. *People leaving. People like her.* That was it! He turned and nodded at the cat. Here was a new way to watch for her while remaining unseen. More promising than the bird idea. And thanks to the garden and its vines, he could lie back and conserve energy at the same time. The cat stared at him for a moment. Then it turned, coiled itself, and bounded back onto the top of the outer wall.

Moonshadow grinned, mouthing "Thank you." Had the creature read his mind? Perhaps the natural rapport between them was even stronger than he had realized. He watched the animal pace busily up and down the wall.

The rain stopped. Moonshadow linked himself with the cat, then lay back in the vines with his eyes closed, seeing only what the cat saw, and conserving his *ki* energy. After a long back stretch, the temple cat relaxed into a lazy, seated hunch, grooming its damp face with one paw as it watched the passersby on the road below its perch.

New voices came from beyond the wall. The air felt freshly scrubbed now and Fushimi was coming back to life. The trickle of people exiting and entering town had doubled in just a few minutes. No one was wasting the break in the rain.

Through the temple cat's eyes Moonshadow studied every woman, girl, and lightly built male passing the wall on their way out of Fushimi. The more he thought about it, the more he was convinced that Yuki would try to sneak out of town this way, blending in with the human traffic as before. In some new disguise, of course. Why, Moonshadow asked himself, did he feel so certain? He smiled. Because it was exactly what *he* would do.

AMBUSH!

O nly another minute passed before he was proved right. Through the beast sight's usual watery veil he spotted her. The first thing his trained eye recognized was the perfectly balanced stride of those skinny long legs. As she approached from the poor street, he could make out her face. His stomach knotted. This was it, his best and maybe only chance to put everything right!

She was now disguised as a girl pilgrim and, judging by the pack on her back, she was definitely leaving town. He smiled at the bedroll she shouldered, knowing what was hidden in there. Yuki had stolen a paper cloak, a straw hat, and even a blue sash that read: PILGRIM BOUND FOR THE SHRINE AT ISE. DONATIONS PLEASE.

He marveled. What audacity! She planned to give him—and everybody else—the slip, wearing exactly the same disguise *he* had worn on the way in. Moonshadow grinned at her boldness. He had to admit, for a girl, she was good, and *that* was a nice touch.

As she neared the wall, he frowned. He knew he wasn't good at this, but why did the energy he was sensing feel different now? He could still feel what he had assumed all along was her presence. But now there was something alongside it, an energy current that hadn't been there before. Was he really sensing something extra, or was the impression just a side effect of her presence growing stronger as she neared him? He shook his head, breaking the link with the cat at the same time. No matter! At least he had found her now and it was all straightforward from here. He'd follow her out of town. Get the plans back. What then? He'd have to work that out as he went along.

Moonshadow leapt up onto the outer wall. The cat was startled and it glared at him but stood its ground. He checked in every direction. Only a small boy, tagging along behind his farmer parents, had seen him land. Moonshadow watched the back of Yuki's hat as she strode away. He'd let her go a little further, then he would spring down and shadow her.

Abruptly she stopped and began looking around. He hunched low. Had she sensed him?

The cat hissed and leapt from the wall. Moonshadow stiffened as he watched it run through the garden and vanish under the bamboo gate. Now he felt it too: not just a vague impression of a *shinobi* presence, but a real sense of *danger*.

Just as he glanced back to the girl, men and horses came rushing at her from all sides. He recognized the four attackers at once. The two men on foot were Jiro, Silver Wolf's pet gangster, and Akira, always the man in black. The other two, on horseback, were the same samurai he had encountered on the castle's high walkway. Moonshadow ground his teeth together with tension. They must have identified her earlier and set this trap. His eyes flicked to Akira. Yes, Mister Black Robe there must have sensed her. He really was the real menace of this little team.

The girl took off her straw hat and threw it aside. She drew her *shinobi* sword, then dropped its bedroll covering to the mud. At the sight of a ready blade, the passing peasants and townsfolk scattered in all directions, some of them screaming.

Her attackers circled her on the wide road. Moonshadow saw the undaunted look on her face. Yuki raised her chin, adopting a proud, warlike stance, and her eyes filled with fire. Moonshadow stared without blinking. She was astonishingly brave.

Thick grey spools lying against the horses' saddles caught his eye. Moonshadow focused on them. Each mounted samurai was carrying a long chain, looped many times.

The tall samurai pulled his beast to a halt then raised a length of chain between his hands. A small, eight-sided iron weight hung at the end. Moonshadow gaped. That type of weighted chain was used to stun, not kill. So they intended to take her alive. Silver Wolf not only wanted his plans back, but answers too. The girl spy would not be treated kindly.

"Now!" Akira shouted. Each samurai dangled his weight a short length beside his horse, then, swaying back and forth in the saddle, set it rotating. As the strips of chain spun and gained momentum, whirring filled the air. The street was empty now apart from the girl and her enemies. Shutters slammed on nearby houses. Word had traveled fast that trouble was brewing, the kind that involved men from the castle and swordplay.

Moonshadow's hands balled into fists. He couldn't let them take her. Suddenly the plans she carried were the last thing on his mind. He didn't know why, but all he cared about right now was rescuing the girl who called herself Yuki. He pulled his backpack to one side and rummaged in it for a percussion-triggered smoke bomb. Then he drew his sword from its hiding place and bounded from the wall to the muddy street below.

The Deathless held his sword out before him. Silently pushing through the vines, he moved away from the wall. He stood tall, stretched, and let out a disappointed sigh.

"So close, runt, so very close," he muttered. The assassin sheathed his sword and listened to the sounds coming from over the wall. Shouts, hoof-stamps, the whirring of the capture chains.

The cruel hand of chance he had just suffered made him shake his head. He had been *seconds* away from ambushing the boy spy. Alone and unexpected, just the way he liked it.

On arrival, his target hadn't sensed him resting inside the garden's thick wall of vines. Or perhaps he had, without knowing what the impression meant? The Deathless knew that his *shinobi* aura was a hard one to detect; its subtlety had helped him creep up on many a skilled foe. He had bided his time, watching the boy nestle into the vines a few paces to his left.

He had thought himself gifted with the best timing and luckiest break ever. Then, just as he'd prepared to make his move, that pesky girl had passed by and somehow, his target had known it. Now, hell itself was breaking loose and the opportunity was lost.

A deep voice the other side of the wall cried, "Who cares? Surround them both!" It was Akira, springing his little trap. The Deathless walked up to the outer wall, then turned and sat down, putting his broad back against it.

"Go ahead, fools," he said to himself. "Take down the girl and have your last try at the boy. You need one another's help. I work alone." He cocked his head to one side, listening. "But feel free to tire him for me first." The Deathless rubbed his sword shoulder. "Soon, young man, we'll dance." He grinned. "Then one must fall."

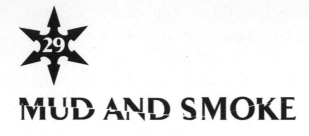

MUD AND SMOKE

W hat are you doing, Nanashi?" The girl gaped at him.

He put his back to hers. "It's Moonshadow," he muttered quickly, raising his sword and pointing its tip at the nearest samurai rider's whirling chain. "We'll settle *our* matter later!" Moonshadow turned and gave her a determined glance. Their eyes met for an instant. "I won't let them take you, Yuki."

"Then I won't let them take you either." Her face glowed with a mix of surprise and delight. "By the way," she added proudly, "it's Snowhawk!" She nodded crisply, then turned her back to his, her expression growing fierce once more.

"I said *surround* them!" Akira growled. "Space yourselves evenly!"

The tallest samurai rode closer, controlling his horse's reins with one hand. He pulled the animal to a sliding halt on the muddy street, then launched the end of his rotating chain at Moonshadow. The eight-sided weight flashed past Snowhawk, grey links noisily snaking out behind it. Moonshadow dropped into a crouch and the weighted whip lashed just above his head as its chain snapped taut. He flicked up the blunt edge of his sword, trying to tangle the chain, but it was quickly yanked out of range. The samurai reeled his chain in, then started the weight spinning again.

Turning fast on his horse, the short samurai moved behind Snowhawk and lined her up with the grey vertical disc of his spinning chain. He lurched forward in the saddle, releasing the weighted end. It flew at her.

"Down!" Moonshadow yelled. Snowhawk threw herself into a forward roll. The weight flicked the end strands of her hair as she tumbled away.

Akira ran to fill a gap in the circle of attackers, raising his sword as he dropped into a combat stance. Its tip pointed at Moonshadow's throat.

"You and me, boy!" Akira shouted confidently. "Come on, just us...how about it?"

Jiro scrambled around the moving circle until he was behind Moonshadow. Moonshadow sensed a presence at his back and turned his head. Jiro raised a *shuriken* in each hand. He waited until Moonshadow glanced back at Akira again, then he hurled the first one.

Out of the corner of his eye, Moonshadow saw Snowhawk's mouth tighten. Her sword rose fast. Abruptly she lunged at him. For a split second he thought it meant betrayal and instinctively raised his own sword. Then he heard the *fff* of a *shuriken* closing on his head from behind and he knew. Moonshadow froze. Snowhawk's blade swished past his head to block the *shuriken* with a loud *clang*. The spent black throwing knife spun away in a high arc, plunging into the walled garden.

Jiro lobbed his second *shuriken*, aiming for Snowhawk. She was ready for it and dodged, gripping Moonshadow's sleeve and pulling him out of harm's way. The *shuriken* streaked near the pair's heads then narrowly missed Akira. It glanced off the wall, close to the assassin's elbow, before spiraling into the mud.

"Do that again, Jiro," Akira shouted with a red face, "and I *will* kill you!"

"Yeah, sure," Jiro called indifferently, taking new *shuriken* from his jacket.

The tall samurai prepared to let fly with his chain once more. His partner made ready to launch a simultaneous attack from a different angle.

"Two at once!" Moonshadow hissed to Snowhawk. "That way!"

He and Snowhawk jumped, as hard and high as they could, in the direction of the wall. The two weighted chains rocketed across each other with an edgy grinding sound, almost tangling right where their targets had stood. The two samurai pulled the chains apart and reeled them in fast.

Snowhawk and Moonshadow landed beside the wall but were given no time to think. Akira rushed them. Jiro raised a *shuriken* in each hand, shuffling sideways as he tried to set up a throwing angle without Akira in the line of fire.

"Take the offensive," Snowhawk grunted. "Push through them to the shrine!"

Moonshadow gave her a nod and then bounded forward to meet Akira, who looked pleased that his foe seemed keen to fight. But as Moonshadow closed in, he stretched out and hacked fast with the tip of his sword, at the same time launching himself into a powerful jump.

Akira was startled by the tricky move and, as he raised a block to Moonshadow's flashing blade, the boy somersaulted over him then hit the ground running. Akira turned and gave chase. Moonshadow dashed alongside the wall for the great red gate of the shrine.

He looked back. Snowhawk had just blocked a *shuriken* attack with her blade and now she was running in a zigzag at Jiro. Jiro grinned and skipped backward, drawing a dagger.

Moonshadow spun about and traded several cuts and blocks with Akira. Then the two faced off, swords extended, each waiting for the other to make a move and, hopefully, a mistake. Moonshadow glanced sideways, curious how Snowhawk was doing.

Jiro had backed away from the girl spy, dagger in one hand, a *shuriken* in the other. The two watched each other now with equally ferocious, scheming eyes. He was preparing to throw, she to block. Another tense standoff.

Hoofs stamped and gouged the mud as the

mounted samurai took up new positions, their chains whirling again. Moonshadow snorted with resolve. This couldn't go on. Eventually, he and Snowhawk would be worn down, then *brought down* with those chains. He sprang backward out of Akira's sword range and caught Snowhawk's eye. She glanced at Jiro's hands, then back at Moonshadow.

When their eyes were briefly locked, Moonshadow mouthed the word *gate*. He held a fist against his belly and flicked his fingers open quickly, suggesting an explosion.

Snowhawk gave a tiny nod, then resumed watching Jiro's twitching *shuriken* hand.

The samurai closed in, this time both targeting Moonshadow. Akira stole a sideways look at them, then stepped back out of the field of fire. Moonshadow's hand flashed into his jacket, fingers closing around the smoke bomb.

"Now!" he shouted. He drew the percussion-triggered pellet and hurled it hard at the ground near Akira's feet. Unsure of what was coming at him, Akira bounded to one side, sword swooping across his belly, ready to block.

The smoke bomb went off with a low *hiss*. Jiro threw his *shuriken*. The samurai launched their chain weights. Moonshadow and Snowhawk each vaulted into the plume of smoke as it quickly expanded along the wall. In seconds it was a dense white cloud.

He heard Snowhawk give a sharp cry of pain. His stomach knotted hard. Had that last *shuriken* found its mark? Through the cloud came two heavy *thuds* as weights hit the wall nearby. The white cloud grew larger still, and Moonshadow could tell his bomb's smokescreen powder was about to run out. Suddenly Snowhawk loomed in front of him. With gritted teeth she pulled a *shuriken* from one shoulder.

"I'm hit," she whispered angrily, "but it's nothing. I can still fight!"

"You in there, girl?" Jiro's mocking voice pierced the white fog. "I got you, didn't I? Oh, that's right…did I forget to mention? I really wanted a win this time, so you know what I did? I had the points of *these shuriken* dipped. In sleeping potion!"

"He's bluffing," Moonshadow hissed. Snowhawk covered her wound, shaking her head.

"Feeling tired yet?" Jiro gave a high-pitched giggle. "Here! Try some more!"

A blindly thrown *shuriken* whizzed through the cloud. It ricocheted off the wall near their heads. The pair bobbed low. Moonshadow gestured quickly.

"Jump for the gate," he panted, speaking into her ear, "the shrine, then *uphill*."

Despite her injury, Snowhawk's face lit up as she grasped his meaning. If they fled uphill to where the streets were both steep *and* muddy, these samurai would have trouble controlling their horses.

Side by side they leapt hard for the shrine gate, half-hidden already by the smoky curtain, just as the tip of Akira's sword sang through the white fog where Moonshadow's head had been.

OUTFLANKED

They ran through the grounds of the shrine, *shuriken* blurring past them. Hurdling over a low fence, the duo tore uphill along a street of fancy homes where the town's wealthy merchants lived. With every footfall they splashed each other with dark mud and water.

Moonshadow saw Snowhawk start to lag behind him as they pounded higher. He muttered a curse on Jiro. The gangster hadn't been bluffing. The potion was affecting her already.

The street ended at the foot of the sake brewery, where the pair ran for the cover of the three massive wooden vats. They crouched together behind a thick upright beam that was part of one vat's support tower. Moonshadow leaned out, peering downhill.

Snowhawk rubbed her shoulder. "I hate being so close to the castle again."

"Me too," he panted heavily, "but under these vats must be the only dry ground left in town. We need to catch our breath here, then lose them before we leave Fushimi, or we'll only wind up fighting them in some field or forest, with a lot fewer places to hide."

"Agreed. Can you see them?" Snowhawk gasped, her eyes gliding left and right.

"No, but we can't relax," he warned her. "They could be flanking us as we speak. There are back lanes you can't see from here. They run from near the shrine to the far side of the brewery. Wait!" He turned his head sharply. "I think I heard a horse!"

Snowhawk grabbed his arm. He looked at her.

"I feel someone behind us," she whispered.

Moonshadow leapt to his feet and turned, raising his sword.

Under the vat farthest away, Akira was striding toward them, his blade at the ready. The man in black. He must have circled behind the brewery, perhaps trying to flush them out.

"So?" Akira raised one eyebrow. "Who will it be

first? Either way, it won't take long!" Moonshadow looked quickly in all directions. Where were the others?

"Run," he whispered to Snowhawk, "back onto the street, head downhill again. Remember about the horses, avoid flat ground." She shook her head. "Go!" he snapped, pushing her.

She hesitated, then crept between the beams that supported the vats. Moonshadow watched her weave past the outermost uprights to the mud before he turned.

"Come on! I'm in the mood now." He gestured to Akira. "Let's get this over with!"

Akira flashed his cold smile. "It was nice never knowing you," he said. He took a deep breath and rushed Moonshadow.

Once he was within sword-reach, Akira dropped to one knee, turning his weapon and hacking hard left to right on a horizontal plane. Moonshadow knew the shin-cutting move and jumped over the flashing blade. As he landed he brought his own sword down fast, aiming for Akira's head, but the experienced foe recovered from his swing with blinding speed. Akira's sword turned, darted up, and blocked Moonshadow's attack.

The *shinobi* swords locked together with a dull ring, then slid noisily down each other's lengths until their square hand guards *clank*ed together. Moonshadow found himself face to face with Akira as each of them tried, leaning in hard, to force the other one back. He knew they both had the same plan: push the foe off, free the sword, and strike at close range.

Moonshadow forced Akira back a step. Akira snarled at him, teeth gnashing with effort. Then Moonshadow heard Snowhawk roar a battle cry out on the street.

"Go on!" Akira's eyes twinkled, his head shone with sweat. "Turn, have a look!"

Ignoring the bait, Moonshadow gave a furious thrust. Akira went with the shove's momentum, pulled his sword free of the clench, and slashed for Moonshadow's neck. Moonshadow narrowly ducked the cut, which lopped off a muddy bundle of his hair. He spun around and darted quickly through the support beams to the street. Moonshadow knew Akira would follow. It didn't matter. This might be his only chance to rejoin Snowhawk.

As his sandals met the mud, he saw his predicament. Snowhawk had fled only a dozen paces downhill before the mounted samurai had appeared, closing on her quickly from one side of the brewery. From the other direction loomed Jiro, his chest heaving from running uphill, a *shuriken* already poised in each of his hands.

Moonshadow cursed him again. Didn't this nuisance *ever* run out of ammunition?

The samurai started whirling their chains as they cut off Snowhawk's escape with their horses. But moving on the steep hillside was no easy task: both animals' hooves slid in the deep mud, making their riders' every maneuver difficult. Moonshadow smiled as he watched the horses struggle. This was good. Now *they* had a handicap. It had been wise coming up here. The sound of the turning chains grew louder. The samurai converged.

"Back to me!" he shouted to Snowhawk. Moonshadow turned to find Akira almost within striking range. But the assassin suddenly stopped, his sword drooping, eyes flicking to *something* behind Moonshadow. Something coming at him, maybe?

Akira jumped back. Moonshadow's instincts told him to duck and as he did, a weight streaked just above his head, dragging a chain behind it.

The weight and its tail of chain narrowly passed the thick upright beam supporting the outermost vat. As the chain grew taut, the weight orbited the support pole and abruptly dropped over the now fully extended chain. The weight swung around and around the chain, tangling in ever-tighter loops.

Moonshadow gave a satisfied grunt. The tallest samurai had now accidentally tied his horse to the tower with his length of chain. The vat sat too low for its rider to simply gallop under and unhook his capture weapon. This was a great opportunity, but it wouldn't last long.

"Push him downhill!" Moonshadow yelled to Snowhawk.

She gave a sharp nod. "My thought exactly!"

Akira bounded forward and sliced for his arm, but Moonshadow dodged clear and ran out onto the hillside, straight for the samurai whose chain had tangled. Snowhawk did the same, her sword's tip swishing for the rider's nearest leg.

The tall samurai panicked as the two spies came at him, raking and stabbing the air, frightening his horse. With his hands full controlling his reins and the chain that was anchored to his saddle, he couldn't draw a sword. Retreat was the only option. His smaller partner looked on helplessly as the tall samurai turned his horse and tried to escape down-hill. With the horse's skittish movements, the chain had regained some slack but now it snapped tight again, jerking the big animal to a skidding halt and almost flinging its rider from his saddle. As the horse scrambled, its hooves slid in the mud and the chain relaxed and then tensed again. The support beam under the outermost vat gave a menacing creak.

Akira glanced up at the chained tower and then ran clear. The horse neighed anxiously, sliding a little downhill, mud covering its hooves. Its chain was wrenched taut again. After more loud creaking, a wet splintering sound came from under the vat. The samurai tried to control his distressed animal, but the horse made as if to bolt downhill, giving the chain its most powerful tug yet. With a thunderous crack the support beam came away from the bottom of the vat.

Moonshadow blinked at the unfolding damage. The thick timber's base had stayed in the ground, but as the horse strained forward its chain dragged the top of the beam out over the street at a sharp angle. The vat above it groaned and one side lurched.

Snowhawk swayed on the spot. Moonshadow ran up to her, snatched a grip on her sleeve, and together they ran downhill, their highly honed balancing skills keeping them upright on the treacherous wet ground. A *shuriken* hurtled past, so they scurried into a zigzag run. Neither looked back until they were halfway down the hill. Then Akira and Jiro intercepted them, one darting in from each side.

Moonshadow and Snowhawk again went back-to-back.

"I feel weak," she whispered to him. "As if I may faint. You should—"

"What?" He elbowed her gently. "Fight these fools on my own? Why must I do all the work?"

A raucous series of cracks and snaps came from the brewery towers. Moonshadow couldn't see exactly what caused the sounds, but glancing uphill he quickly placed their other two opponents.

The tall samurai, his horse still attached to the beam, was hunched over his saddle, trying to release the chain. About twenty paces from him, his partner's horse had lost its footing completely and fallen onto its side, pinning its rider in the mud by one leg.

Jiro held up his usual *shuriken* in each hand. "My last pair! Let's see you dodge these *up close*!" He made for the duo, his every step spattering his clothes with mud.

Akira dashed in also, his steps lighter, every move more agile and controlled. His look of resolve showed that he too planned to end the game now.

From above came a great roaring *crraacckk!* It was

followed by a series of wet, heavy *thuds* and *thunks*, then splintering sounds and the damp tinkling of bamboo and planks tumbling together.

"What's that?" Jiro scowled. "Some new *shinobi* trick?" He sneaked a look uphill, but was afraid to take his eyes from Snowhawk for too long. "Something's falling!"

Akira kept his gaze locked on Moonshadow. Moonshadow decided to take a chance. With lightning speed he glanced up at the towers then back to his opponent.

What he saw made his blood run cold. The outermost brewery vat had toppled from its weakened tower. It had broken open, dumping enough pale rice pulp to fill a pond, and now it was rolling downhill on its side. Round wooden tower braces and long pipes made from giant bamboo had also been torn free. They tumbled downhill around and behind it.

The four of them stood in the path of the oncoming debris. Moonshadow gripped his sword tightly, eyeing Akira.

"The vat's fallen; it's coming!" he warned.

"Nice try!" Akira smiled. "If I look away, you'll cut me!"

A deep shout and wet rumbling from above made them all look. Despite his best efforts to avoid it, the edge of the rolling vat had clipped the tallest samurai, flinging him from his scrambling horse into the mud. The vat was bearing down on them now with only seconds to spare. Jiro shrieked as they scattered. Snowhawk plucked up the last of her strength and bounded after the gangster. Startled as she landed behind him, Jiro threw himself into the mud and rolled hard to escape both the vat and the reach of her sword. Moonshadow leapt out of the vat's path and was surprised when Akira also jumped high and fast. The vat thundered past them downhill, losing planks as it rolled. Moonshadow looked around and quickly bounded again, barely avoiding a tumbling tower brace. Akira saw a thick length of bamboo pipe hurtling for him and rather than jump once more he cut it in two. A great slimy film of pale rice pulp trailed the debris down the hill, expanding as it came. An odor of rotting plants filled the air.

Once the four had regained their footing, they watched the vat finally come apart like a ruptured barrel. Blocking the street at the bottom of the hill, it crumbled noisily into a pile of gnarled timber and iron hooping. With *whump*s and rattles, the rolling bamboo pipes and tower braces caught up, landing all around the straggly heap.

Moonshadow twirled back to face Akira. The

distance between them was greater now. He had time to turn, make sure that Snowhawk was safe. Moonshadow looked and wished he hadn't.

Snowhawk staggered, her sword extended toward Jiro, her arm faltering. Moonshadow gasped as her legs buckled and she collapsed into the mud. Jiro ran forward, drawing his dagger, looming over her. Moonshadow felt his heart skip several beats.

"No, Jiro," Akira shook his head firmly. "Our Lord was adamant. He wants her *alive*!"

Moonshadow ground his teeth. That treacherous hill and the happy accident of the vat had handed them an advantage, reducing the odds from four against two to even. Snowhawk's collapse had just snatched it away again. Now it was two against one.

"In that case, it'll be *me* who brings you down!" Sheathing his dagger, Jiro stepped forward and hurled his last two *shuriken* at Moonshadow in rapid succession. Moonshadow's sword streaked from its ready position to block the first missile with a loud *shing*. The *shuriken* blurred away downhill. Moonshadow checked himself quickly. He wasn't wounded. So where had that second one gone?

He glanced at Akira, only to find the assassin examining a brand new slash high on the sleeve of his black jacket. Jiro's second *shuriken* had clipped him. Had it cut his clothing only, or actually broken the skin? Would he soon fall, like Snowhawk?

"Excuse me one moment, will you, boy?" Akira gave Moonshadow a polite bow, then moved around him cautiously. Suddenly he turned and paced for Jiro. "I warned you!" he growled, sheathing his sword.

Jiro sniggered amiably as if it was all a joke, but he held out his dagger. "Hey now...come on, let's not get crazy here...the kid there's the enemy, right?" Akira kept coming. Jiro's face hardened. "Oh, like that then, is it? Think I'm afraid of you, old man? Man with the big reputation! Your sword may be longer than my knife, but *what—*"

Moonshadow followed the gangster's stare. To his astonishment, Akira had pulled a *shuriken* of his own from his black robe. He held it high. It wasn't star-like, as Jiro's were. It had only four long, thin points.

"A professional," Akira said coolly, "needs only *one.*"

"Don't do it!" Jiro backed away. "I'm not in the contract!"

"Gangster scum," Akira sniffed. "Only *shinobi* or samurai deserve to die by the sword."

Jiro's bottom lip trembled and he talked faster

than ever. "Kill me, with this kid still alive and untouched, and you'll answer to Silver Wolf; *you know you will!*"

Moonshadow glanced at Snowhawk, then took a step sideways in her direction, keeping his eyes on Akira's *shuriken*. If the assassin noticed him going to her aid, he might just spin about and launch that thing at *him* instead of Jiro. Moonshadow snuck in a few more quick steps. If only they would go on arguing, or better still actually fight, he could reach her...

Akira suddenly stopped, making Moonshadow freeze on the spot. The man in black gave a frustrated sigh. "You're right, killing you would be a mistake." With amazing speed he hurled the *shuriken* at Jiro. The gangster tried to block it with his dagger, but it flashed under his blade and straight into his knee. The *whump* of its impact made Moonshadow wince. "But I *can* take you out of the game!" Akira snarled.

Jiro dropped his dagger and looked down at the *shuriken* sticking out of his kneecap. He started to pull his stupid grin, then his face twisted with pain.

"That really hurts," Jiro said hoarsely, "Dirty trick, getting me with my own weapon of choice—" Jiro's eyes rolled back in his head as he fainted, falling hard into the mud. Moonshadow's mouth twisted as he considered Jiro's injury. He wouldn't walk for *months*.

Akira turned to Moonshadow, drawing his sword as he spoke. "Now let's end this as we should: a contest of equals. My name is Akira."

"I know." Moonshadow gave a quick bow. "I am Moonshadow."

His enemy's eyes twinkled. "Like the sword move?" Akira almost smiled.

"Exactly," Moonshadow said.

"Then I invite you," Akira baited, "to *try* your signature technique against me." His face lit up menacingly. "But be warned: I've seen it before."

"So had the last man I used it on." Moonshadow readied his blade.

A moment of silence passed before they rushed each other.

MOONSHADOW

The hillside rang with the sounds of clashing steel as Moonshadow and Akira exchanged a flurry of strikes and counters. There were many near misses, but no one was cut. Panting, they jumped back from one another. Moonshadow swallowed. Akira appeared to be every bit as skilled with a sword as he. How to defeat him, without going all the way and taking his life? He concentrated, clearing his mind, thinking quickly. What would Mantis do *now*, if *he* was fighting this enemy in the open, in a daylight duel? There could be no exploiting the cover of shadow this time. And as for being unpredictable yet again...how? Picturing his trainer's soft but cunning eyes inspired him.

Every duel is a gamble, a contest of wits. Figure out what your enemy expects, Mantis would often say, *then do the opposite.* Moonshadow narrowed his eyes thoughtfully. Many dueling defenses began with the swordsman in a low stance, or kneeling on the ground. From that position, Moonshadow might launch any one of thirty techniques. The last one Akira would expect was the very one they had just bantered about. His signature technique. But if Akira read the signals fast enough, and guessed their meaning, Moonshadow was finished. He scowled. *Every duel is a gamble.*

Moonshadow paced backward away from Akira, then rummaged in his back-mounted bedroll. Akira watched him intently, frowning. Moonshadow took his sword's scabbard from the bedroll, sheathed his blade, then carefully mounted it on his left hip. He turned and faced the castle, sinking to his knees, rocking back on his heels in the mud.

"No *shinobi* tricks now." Akira took a step forward. "This is a clash of *swords!*"

Approaching at an angle, Akira strode toward Moonshadow, who remained on his heels, seeming to ignore his advancing enemy. Moonshadow rested his palms on his thighs and stared off beyond the distant moat. His eyes grew dreamy and he seemed unprepared for combat. Worse still, by kneeling on the ground he had given Akira a height advantage. Akira eyed him suspiciously, then, deciding to take the opportunity anyway, he accelerated into a charge. His sword swung up and over his head, ready for a powerful descending cut.

His target let him come. At the last possible, critical moment, Moonshadow grasped his sword with one hand and his sheath with the other and turned his knees, using the mud to slide around so he could face his attacker. In a flash he rose up onto one foot. Planting his weight firmly, he drew the pommel of his sword toward Akira.

The man in black bore down on him, sword poised to fall. Moonshadow sprang into a low angular stance, his blade and scabbard parting in an explosive fast draw. His sword rose with lightning speed, swishing as it traced the shape of a crescent moon. The first third of its blade bit into Akira's raised forearms before he could swing his strong downward cut.

On impact Moonshadow's sword gave a double *clunk* which told him that under those long black sleeves, Akira's forearms were protected by armor.

No *shinobi* tricks? Moonshadow cursed under his breath. Akira had come prepared for anything with a trick of his own.

He heard Snowhawk stir and let out a cry of pain. His throat began to close with tension, but he willed himself to concentrate. If he lost his focus now, Akira would slay him, then take Snowhawk to Silver Wolf and the unthinkable would befall her.

With deep scraping sounds armor and sword ground together. In a split second Moonshadow relived his last duel with Groundspider. But that had been a rehearsal; this was life and death. Akira's cold eyes bored into him. Moonshadow avoided them and stared at Akira's sword shoulder. A harder target than the man's head, but—

Taking a deep breath, he made his decision.

He set his teeth and pushed with everything he had, channeling all his strength and body weight into his sword to shove Akira back as he had under the brewery tower. He needed but a small gap between them in order to pull back his blade and strike with decisive speed. Moonshadow roared as he finished the great push.

Rammed backward with unexpected power, Akira's feet slid and he lost his balance on the muddy ground. As he narrowly avoided stumbling, the gap

Moonshadow had needed briefly opened. He took a long single stride then struck once, hard, with a powerful cut aimed straight for his enemy's sword shoulder. His weapon's tip met Akira's jacket and there was a dull *snick*, the sound of a blade cutting fabric. Akira shuddered and both fighters froze on the spot. Moonshadow stood fast, watching, with his sword extended and its tip buried in Akira's shoulder.

Akira stood motionless, gripping his own weapon tightly, eyes fixed with concentration. Then he stepped back, pulling his shoulder clear of Moonshadow's sword. Akira swayed. His weapon tumbled from his hands. He sank to one knee in the mud.

"Congratulations," Akira said tersely, clutching his shoulder. "Resorting to the obvious! Crafty pup, you pulled it off."

"Thanks." Moonshadow shook off his sword and sheathed it on his hip.

Akira closed his eyes. Pressing his wound with both hands, he fell sideways into the mud. Soft rain began to fall. Akira slowly scooped a handful of mud and used it to stanch the bleeding from the cut in his shoulder.

His chest heaving, Moonshadow wiped sweat and grime from his eyes and blinked at his fallen enemy. He'd been sorely tempted to kill Akira, but now he understood what Mantis had been trying to tell him. Whether done with so-called honor or not, a wise man found no glory in killing. Enemy or not, Akira was brave and skillful—a professional spy, like Moonshadow, cunning and inventive. He had simply been on the other side, that was all. Moonshadow had been forced to put *him* out of the game, just as Akira had Jiro, but he had not scattered this grain of life.

He could hear his teacher's voice in his head. *Even the sword that serves justice is still an instrument of death.* Moonshadow nodded. To live with regrets as Mantis did was the burden of all warriors with true hearts and minds. Regrets! At least so far, he had created none. Mantis would be proud of him, and happy for him.

"Don't try to follow me, Akira-San," Moonshadow bowed to his foe. "In overcoming you, I was simply lucky. But you're wounded now, so next time, I won't need luck." He smiled grimly, his eyes flicking to the crumpled form of Jiro. "By the way, Akira-San, nice *shuriken* throw!"

Akira stared at up at him thoughtfully for a moment, then slowly, wincing as he worked, unfastened one of his armored forearm guards. Akira threw it at Moonshadow's feet before giving a pained nod. "I appreciate your good manners," he grunted.

"So take it. Something to remember me by…until we next meet."

Moonshadow picked up the forearm guard. A heavy single scar ran across it. He smiled at the dent, his own handiwork, then slipped the guard over his left hand, bowing again to Akira as he pulled its fastenings tight. "Thank you."

The wounded man half-nodded, closed his eyes, and went on stanching the blood flowing from his cut.

Moonshadow ran to Snowhawk. Raising her from the mud, he tried to sit her up. She was a deadweight, but breathing. Her eyelids fluttered. Moonshadow checked over his shoulder. Akira lay still, gripping his cut shoulder tightly. His face was drawn with pain. He was no longer a threat.

Feet splashed the mud behind him. Moonshadow turned his head to the sounds. A stooped town watchman with grey hair was struggling up the hill, using his closed paper umbrella as a walking stick.

"Young sir," the man called anxiously, "is it over? Is it safe now?" He looked at the debris and injured bodies strewn on the muddy hillside. "What a mess you've made of our town, that is…well, what I mean to say…thank the gods you're unhurt!"

Moonshadow fished quickly in his belt with one hand and pulled out a string of silver coins. He caught the town watchman's eye, then threw him the money.

"That's for the damage. And to pay a doctor. See to the man in black." Moonshadow pointed at Akira, then sighed, nodding at the motionless Jiro. "The gangster, too." He looked around for the two castle samurai. One was pinned under his fallen horse, the other covered by debris. If they lived, their warlord master, if he kept to any code at all, would see to their care.

"Not this young lady also?" The watchman frowned.

"I'll see to her. If anyone from the castle asks you, tell them we took the road to the highway." Moonshadow flashed him a stern look. "*Understand?*"

The watchman tested the weight of the coins with one hand. His wrinkled face lit up. Moonshadow had thrown him a great deal of money.

"It will *all* be done, young sir," he said eagerly, "before all the *kami*, all the old gods, I swear. Oh, and to Amida Buddha himself too, I promise!"

Moonshadow looked down at Snowhawk as the watchman turned away. Under his breath he prayed, "Please, Lord Buddha, don't guide this one to the next life yet."

Tangled, dirty hair hung over Snowhawk's face.

She was breathing, but in a fitful, half-drugged sleep, in the grip of the potion. At least, Moonshadow thought, if it was of a common formula, its effects would be short-lived. She would need water, lots of it. He sighed heavily—partly with relief because she was alive, but also for what he had to do, regardless of her condition. Or wishes.

He gently untangled the leather thong from her hair and slipped it over her head. Snowhawk opened one eye. She saw the thong dangling from his fist and tried without success to raise one hand.

"Nooo," Snowhawk pleaded, her voice low and weak.

"Sorry." Moonshadow put the thong around his neck and fed the plans into his jacket.

"If I return without them, I'm as good as dead," Snowhawk whispered. "That is the custom of my clan: on every mission, death is the price for failure!"

"You're not returning," he said firmly, "with *or* without them!" He gripped her shoulders tightly. "My people don't kill agents for failure, they retrain them. You're coming with me."

"All shadow clans kill spies who fail," she muttered. "Or make them kill themselves."

"Maybe so," Moonshadow paused, then decided to take another big gamble. "But I am not of a shadow clan. I am of the Grey Light, the shogun's secret service. Come with me; let me beg my masters that you might join us. Do *your* masters deserve your loyalty? They might have trained you well, but one day they'll slay you for a mistake. We never would."

He struggled to his feet, dragging Snowhawk to hers. Her legs buckled immediately and he barely held her up.

"They will hunt me," she gasped. "And besides... even if I do try...try to have a new life...they are all I've ever known. Perhaps...even *they* deserve...a goodbye at least...only some of them...maybe, I could just..." Her eyelids fell.

"Forget that!" he said stubbornly. "Let them believe you dead, or my prisoner. I can see you're confused! But do you want to live, or not?"

Moonshadow looked into her face. She opened one eye, gave a faint smile, then fell back to sleep. He threw her over his shoulder and started across the hillside.

With the fighting over, shutters were opening along the streets that faced the battlefield. Wary-faced locals reappeared, inspecting the damage and the wounded. As he moved carefully through the mud, Moonshadow's eyes quickly swept the hill.

The tallest samurai's horse swayed in an exhausted

hunch, flanks shining, head down. After being swatted from his saddle by the edge of the tumbling vat, its rider had been buried by debris that had followed the vat downhill. To Moonshadow's amazement, the samurai was alive. Moonshadow's sharp ears could make out the warrior's groans as two brewery workers started tugging at the tower brace and pipes that half-covered him. Moonshadow shook his head. The spongy mud had probably saved him from being crushed, but he would have broken arms and ribs at the very least.

His colleague, the smaller samurai, was being freed from beneath his fallen horse. A muscular farmer and three women were helping the exhausted animal to stand, while a merchant's laborer dragged the samurai clear. The smaller samurai's leg looked broken.

Moonshadow heard hoofs thrumming loudly on wooden planks, so he peered over the moat to the castle's main gate. Two by two, a column of men rode out, perhaps twenty samurai in all, the leading pair carrying spears.

He scrambled away as fast as the mud would allow. Carrying the now drowsy, mumbling girl, Moonshadow ran the length of the rich merchants' street. When he reached the end of the road and the town itself, he slipped unseen into a lane between two houses, then out, across a thin track and into a dense pine forest.

Two new problems nagged at his mind as he hurried on, teeth locked together hard with the effort of carrying Snowhawk.

First, would the Grey Light Order accept Snowhawk, make her one of their own? If she turned to them, would they ever fully trust one who had betrayed her own shadow clan? And what of his part in her defection? He was breaking rules, violating protocols of secrecy, true, but she also represented a great opportunity for his order, and therefore for the shogun. If Snowhawk truly turned, she would be able to tell them much about their secret enemies, perhaps even about the rebellion!

He thought of Eagle's wisdom, Mantis's compassion, and Heron's caring heart. They just might do it! To save her life, it was worth taking the risk and, if all else failed, he would plead with them to have the White Nun visit and assess Snowhawk. The White Nun's astonishing insight would tell his masters what his heart already knew: Snowhawk was an unmet friend, both to him and to the Grey Light Order. It was destiny, the kind of unexpected twist of fate that Brother Eagle had tried explaining to him, and he felt it from the pit of his stomach to the crown of his head. Once she was conscious, he would try to win her cooperation with his plan, to convince her to take the risk. He prayed she would listen, that she would trust him enough to gamble everything on his judgment.

His second nagging concern was intangible. What had he forgotten? There was *something*, lurking at the edge of his memory, some unresolved matter. With his mind so full of the girl and her needs right now, it would not reveal itself to him.

He had the plans. For now at least, his foes were neutralized. He was even turning an enemy agent. But what was the stone left unturned? Was it one that could crush him if he didn't identify it quickly?

The soft rain stopped. At the top of the first rise, Moonshadow set Snowhawk down gently under a wide, towering pine tree. Curled on a thick bed of pine needles, she snored contentedly while he caught his breath and looked out over Fushimi for the last time. No one appeared to be following. Sounds came from deep inside the town; muddy galloping, a gruff samurai shouting orders, but trees and buildings hid the activity.

Moonshadow saw a trace of nearby movement and he leaned forward, squinting hard at it. He grinned. Could he believe his eyes? The temple cat! It stood on a low stone wall near the mouth of the lane, staring in his direction. Saying farewell, perhaps? Moonshadow shook his head. Perhaps destiny had granted him *two* unmet friends. But there was no room now on his shoulders; this one he would have to leave behind.

He shouldered Snowhawk again and struck out for the rendezvous point, but anxiety clutched at him as he pressed on. He grumbled inwardly, hating this feeling.

What was it? What thread had he left untied?

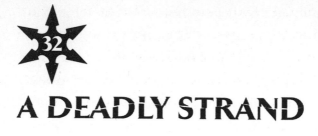

A DEADLY STRAND

Moonshadow struggled uphill. As the pines thinned out and white rocky outcrops appeared, he knew the rendezvous point was not far away. He put Snowhawk down beside a thin stream that cut through the rocky shelf.

With the bamboo water phial from his pack, he wet her face, neck, and wrists, reviving her enough to take a drink. Moonshadow watched Snowhawk drain the remaining water so eagerly that half of it spilled down her chin. He refilled the small bamboo beaker again and again, for Snowhawk was remarkably thirsty. The more she drank, the more alert she became. After drinking several phials of the icy mountain water, she crawled to the stream itself and drank even more. As she quenched her thirst, he studied the surrounding terrain. Between two rather stunted pine trees, Moonshadow spotted the mouth of a small chalk cave.

At last Snowhawk sat up unaided, wiping her mouth. She opened her eyes wide, then looked at Moonshadow. He could tell her head was clearing, but it was also obvious that the potion had left her seriously weakened.

"Welcome back." He smiled at her. "Just in time. I would have had trouble carrying you over this last stretch." He pointed uphill. "If the map I memorized wasn't monkey-stained, just over that ridge lies a rocky gorge. This stream probably feeds into the river that runs through it. The opposite bank of that gorge is where we'll be met."

"Monkey-stained?" Snowhawk rubbed her eyes. "What kind of clan do you work for?"

"Forget it." He grinned. "While you get your legs back, we're going to rest a little and talk about that." He turned and pointed to the cave. "In there, for safety." She peered at the cave mouth, looked thoughtful for a moment, then nodded. He held out his hand. "Besides, either we rest now, or *you* carry *me*."

Snowhawk raised her chin. "Glad you realize that I could...easily."

Moonshadow chuckled. "I guess like me, you grew up pressing a rice-straw dummy overhead fifty times a day."

As he pulled her to her feet, Snowhawk blinked at him dramatically. "*Fifty* times?"

"That's right." Moonshadow filled his chest proudly.

"Fifty!" She gave a weary sigh, shaking her head as they moved off. "Is that all?"

He pulled a frown but said nothing more.

They struggled together to the chalk cave, which turned out to be about half the size of his rented room in Fushimi. Moonshadow set her down carefully, wary of the low, irregular ceiling, then sagged to the chalk-peppered earth beside her, rubbing his aching thighs so their muscles wouldn't go into spasm.

"Remember what I told you?" He looked earnestly at Snowhawk. "If you want to join us, the Grey Light Order—well, if they let you, which I believe they will—you'll never have to fear being killed by your own people, only by an enemy in the field. Everyone, samurai, *shinobi*, merchant or farmer, lives with *that* risk anyway!"

Snowhawk was silent for some time, appearing to weigh his words. Then she cleared her throat. "Very well. Tell me about them. If you truly trust me, and want me to trust you too, then tell me of the Grey Light Order. Not what they do. *Who they are.*"

Moonshadow took a deep breath. His convictions about her had better be right, he thought. Slowly at first, he described his trainers one by one, growing more open and daring with his disclosures as he went on. He cautiously watched Snowhawk's shifting expressions as he told her of those special conversations and moments in which he had truly come to know each of his teachers. *Who they were, not what they did*. She laughed at Moonshadow's stories of Groundspider; at his practical jokes, perverse pride in his size and appetite, and utter inability to cross moats using *mizu gumo*. She fell silent, then nodded solemnly as he recounted Eagle's words concerning the unforeseeable hand of destiny and the importance of trusting one's instincts.

"That you belong with us, and should come home with me now," Moonshadow told her, "these are probably the strongest instincts I've ever felt."

Snowhawk glanced at him, tears welling in her eyes. "Home?" she said. "I am of Clan Fuma. They are powerful and skilled, but I have *never* thought of their mountain fortress as *home*." She wiped one eye with a knuckle and looked away. "Until perhaps now...now, that I have the chance to escape them. Forgive me, I don't know what I'm feeling. One moment, anger and fear. The next—" She groaned. "Can one feel homesick for a brutal world? Or have any sense of obligation to it? Such thoughts are surely madness. They don't matter." Snowhawk took control of her breathing. "Tell me more. *Please*."

He nodded and went on. She was astonished and clearly impressed when he revealed that Badger, the archivist and arch-curmudgeon, was in fact the lauded scholar Hosokawa, who had turned his back on fame over a matter of conscience. Snowhawk shook her head, evidently fascinated, as he told of the wild man that Mantis had been and the truer warrior he had become through acknowledging his regrets and embracing compassion. Finally, when he spoke of discussing loneliness that day in the sunlit garden, and of all that Heron meant to him, Snowhawk hung her head in grim silence.

"We live lives," Moonshadow said slowly, "that simple folk invent fables about. But we are like anyone else, really. We too need friends." He paused, searching for words. "Otherwise our paths...powerful as they are...wind up being empty." Snowhawk gave a half-nod. "Some days I think I would trade my skills, all of them, for a regular life with one identity, no enemies..." — he stared at her — "and just one true friend my age. Since leaving the orphanage, I've never had one."

Snowhawk looked away.

Moonshadow put his hand on her shoulder, biting his lip, unsure what to say or do next.

Snowhawk cleared her throat and shrugged.

"I knew you were brave in combat," Snowhawk sniffed, "but I see now that you also have another kind of courage. I have heard your words, and I will try to be as brave." She rubbed her nose with the back of her sleeve. "I've never heard of a shadow clan like your people. I *will* come with you. I will throw myself on their mercy. What happens then" — she raised her chin proudly and a flash of tenacity lit her eyes — "is up to destiny."

Moonshadow broke into a wide, relieved grin. "I'll help you train," he said excitedly, "help you learn Grey Light Order ways..."

"If they take me in." Her hopeful smile turned sly. "And if you can keep up with me."

"Very funny." Moonshadow raised one eyebrow. "We'll see how fast *you* can cross a moat!"

Moonshadow let them both recover for another

ten minutes, then they left the cave and pressed on together, side by side, up the hill and over the boulder-studded ridge. Thrilled and relieved as he was at Snowhawk's decision, he continued to be plagued by the unsettling idea that he had forgotten something. The gorge appeared below them.

"Yes," Snowhawk said wearily, taking big gulps of air. Then she gripped his sleeve. "I'm still a little confused. It must be the potion. But I think I sense someone. A *shinobi*." She shook her head, tossing mud-streaked hair. "I *think*."

"Well, good!" Moonshadow nodded. "Unless they've been delayed somehow, what you feel must be my people!"

He studied the gorge. It was perhaps a hundred paces wide and forded by a narrow rope bridge, the kind that could only be crossed in single file. The four load-bearing ropes suspending the bridge looked worn, parts of them frayed, but overall the bridge appeared sturdy enough. There was nobody on the far side of the gorge. His Grey Light comrades would be hiding, keeping under cover until they recognized him.

The sky was clearing now but he still heard water; rapids roared below the bridge where the jagged stone walls of the gorge became narrow.

He peered into the depths below. Not a desirable place to fall, Moonshadow thought. It was a long drop, and one's head might clip the unforgiving walls on the way down. Down into the path of a great weight of water, a million *kan* maybe, of angry, surging river. Which for final fun, he noted, was dotted with sharp boulders, many hidden.

Snowhawk pulled on his arm and gestured behind them. Strolling smugly down from the ridge, as if it had every right to be there, was a familiar animal.

"A temple cat? All the way out here?" she smiled. "Has someone adopted us?"

"I don't blame you for following," Moonshadow told the cat as it came, purring, up to his feet. "Fushimi's a nice place to visit, but I wouldn't want to live there either!" He chuckled at his own joke, then turned to Snowhawk. "You spoke of adoption? Well, who could have predicted this? Looks like I'm one orphan who's taking home *two* orphans of his own."

"If any of us make it to your home." The color had drained out of her face. She pointed down at the rope bridge. Moonshadow's eyes flew to it. His mouth fell open in surprise. A dense cloud of white smoke was billowing in the center of the bridge, twisting as it plumed wider, hiding the ropes and boards and whoever was inside the cloud.

"What's Groundspider playing at now?" Moonshadow frowned. "This is no time for a smoke-bomb signal!"

Snowhawk gasped. "It's no signal. It's not your people." She gripped her stomach. "Now I know what I'm sensing...." Her voice became a terrified whisper. "A powerful enemy!"

"What?" Moonshadow blinked with confusion. What sorcery was this? Had Akira made a miraculous recovery, then somehow overtaken them?

As updrafts from the gorge quickly thinned the smoke cloud, a silhouette became visible in the middle of it. Then a strong single puff tore away the last shreds of the white veil. Moonshadow felt Snowhawk stiffen at his side as a dark, solid figure was revealed, looming in the center of the bridge.

Motionless. Waiting. Standing tall and proud, and wearing a distinctive headdress.

With a shudder Moonshadow realized what he had forgotten. Some part of his mind had been trying to warn him, but his excitement over Snowhawk's defection had stifled its voice. One enemy, known to be in Fushimi, had remained unaccounted for.

Until now. The most lethal of them all. The man they said could not be killed.

"Oh no," Moonshadow muttered. "Not here, not now…"

They were in no shape to face such a mighty foe, and there was no guarantee that help was coming. This monster had announced his presence with ominous flair and great confidence. Had he already killed Groundspider and the others?

"Run," Snowhawk hissed, tugging at Moonshadow's sleeve. "Come on, it's downhill; we'll turn back, run hard, and just maybe—"

Moonshadow couldn't answer her. Instead he stared, unblinking and paralyzed, at their lurking enemy. After a long silence, he finally forced out the two words echoing over and again in his mind.

"*The Deathless.*"

His own voice made him want to cringe. It had never sounded so weak or fearful.

THE GREATEST
CHALLENGE

There he waited, arms folded, staring up at them. Moonshadow and Snowhawk exchanged tense looks. They both knew whom they faced.

"I see," The Deathless shouted, "that you didn't have the decency to fight each other after all! No matter. Just give me those plans and you can go."

"Don't trust him," Snowhawk said quickly. "He murdered his own master once he had—" She realized that Moonshadow was about to fight The Deathless and stopped herself.

"Once he had the secret of immunity to blades?"

Moonshadow scowled at the nemesis waiting on the bridge. "Don't worry, I know what I'm up against." He patted his backpack. "No time to put on the armor, but maybe I can wing him first with a *shuriken*."

"Forget that," Snowhawk said firmly. "My trainers told me: he *catches shuriken*."

Moonshadow swung his pack to the ground. Keeping his eyes on the bridge, he dropped to one knee and rummaged in it quickly. "He can't catch what he can't see."

"What are you talking about?" Snowhawk shook her head.

"You'll see," he answered with forced confidence, "but if all goes well, *he* won't."

The cat meowed, brushing between Moonshadow's legs as he stood up. He nodded at it, making himself sound brave and cheerful. "If you're going to butt in, *you* can fight him!" Turning to conceal his actions from his foe down on the bridge, Moonshadow deftly hid several small objects in his jacket. Snowhawk watched him with a dubious frown.

But despite his plan, Moonshadow's heart was quickly becoming a war drum in his chest once more. This would be a harder match than facing Akira; if he couldn't hang on to his inner calm, to clear thinking, this enemy would finish him quickly. To survive such a foe would call for more cunning than he had ever shown. And it still might not be enough. He made a final attempt at bravado. "If only he'd just go away, then I could spare him!"

"You can't face him alone." Snowhawk swallowed. "I can't let you."

He squeezed her hand and said, "You're still too affected by the potion to fight well. So I stand a better chance if I only have to watch out for me. If he kills me, then, as you said, *run*." He saw resistance in her face. "I mean it! If I fall, you run, or he'll sell you to Silver Wolf."

She bit her bottom lip, nodding as he let go and turned away.

With each step his fear grew greater. Desperate to control it, Moonshadow whispered to himself as he strode to face the greatest challenge of his mission. Of his life.

"Gather, tidy, and align your ways, for they bring karma," he recited with nervous speed as he descended into the gorge. "Cleanse any lies made this day, scatter not one grain of life." He swallowed as Snowhawk had, almost choking on his terror. This time, he need not worry about taking life. This...*creature* could not be killed! He mounted the bridge, its short wooden planks shifting under his feet. "To end this path in happiness," he finished off the *furube* sutra with an effort, "seek peace within your mind!"

"Aw!" The Deathless called as Moonshadow approached. "I hear you prepare, so you must come to fight! Unwise, runt! Would you not rather give up the plans and *live?*"

"My name is Moonshadow, you who are called The Deathless." Moonshadow tried to sound casual but avoided his enemy's soulless eyes. "And deathless or not, yes, I come to fight."

The Deathless gave a low, sinister laugh. "Tell me, was that not one of the teachings of the first level that you just recited? How quaint! I would show you something from the ninth level, but if you won't give up the plans, then it's urgent that I kill you instead."

A meow came from just behind Moonshadow. The Deathless peered around him.

"The temple cats of Fushimi are both odd and starved," the killer marveled. "Look! It has a tail! So it is a freak and a girl who will witness your passing, *Moonshadow.*" He threw his head back and laughed. "Why does the beast join us? It looks hungry. Perhaps it intends to feast on you once our business here is done!"

Moonshadow's heart seemed to beat in his mouth now. He summoned up his dwindling shard of courage and drew his sword. He stepped closer. "That's unlikely, since they don't eat the living."

"Hah! You have spirit!" The Deathless sniggered as he drew the blade from its sheath on his back. "But it won't save you."

Moonshadow stepped forward quickly, one hand flashing into his jacket then out again. Using his drawn sword to help him balance, he leaned forward and, with a grunt and great force, launched a *shuriken* straight for the head of his enemy.

The black blur muttered through the air, its throaty sound distorting inside the gorge's rocky walls. At the last possible moment, The Deathless moved, tilting his head minutely to one side to let the *shuriken* narrowly pass him. It arced out of sight and down into the rapids below.

Moonshadow bounded closer, his throwing arm whip-cracking the air again as he launched another missile, this one silent and streaking low. The Deathless swung his sword protectively in front of his legs, but the incoming object was no *shuriken*, nor was it aimed to hit him at all.

Striking the bridge boards between The Deathless's feet, Moonshadow's smoke bomb blazed into life, its pale cloud erupting instantly. As the softly huffing white wall plumed high enough to cover The Deathless's face, Moonshadow drew another *shuriken*, then another, hurling each in rapid succession. They *whirred* through the center of the cloud.

He leapt back, raising his sword between tightly clenched hands. Moonshadow watched the gorge's updrafts start to disperse the false mist.

He froze, leaned forward, and squinted. There was no silhouette this time!

The cloud dispersed to reveal an empty bridge. Moonshadow blinked.

His forehead creased. Was this good or bad news? Had he somehow *done it*? Had he taken down The Deathless with a blind *shuriken* throw—through *shinobi* fog—and sent him tumbling down into the rapids? For a moment, he almost let himself believe it.

"Watch out!" he heard Snowhawk shout. The ropes shook, and boards pitched beneath his feet.

The cat let out a sharp hiss and leaped from the end of the bridge to the safety of solid ground. Two dark outlines blurred up into the edge of Moonshadow's vision and it took him a half breath to realize what they were: part of a figure, appearing feet-first. Moonshadow twisted around. With impossible agility, The Deathless finished his swing from his hiding spot under the bridge, over the main outer rope, and straight at him.

Moonshadow hoisted his sword to block, but it was too late. The Deathless's feet slammed into his ribs and Moonshadow reeled backward, wheezing, to land against one of the bridge's main support ropes and its thinner crosstie.

He saw The Deathless's sword flash down at him and with a sharp *thrang* he blocked its hard strike just in time with the blunt edge of his own weapon. A flash of blue sparks crackled between the blades.

The Deathless nimbly cuffed with his foot in a strong sweep from right to left, dragging Moonshadow's ankles together then off the foot-boards of the narrow bridge. Jolted, his feet dangling, Moonshadow cursed.

Only two ropes, creaking and rubbing and stretched tightly across his back, kept him from falling.

He flailed with his sword, trying to regain balance, but The Deathless seized on the chance to stamp hard, pinning Moonshadow's blade to the boards with one foot. Moonshadow's feet thrashed in space above the roaring rapids.

The Deathless hovered over him, raising his blade for a decisive strike. Moonshadow calculated at blinding speed. What a great choice! His weapon was pinned, and he hung like a struggling fly in a spider's web, so he had two options: let his enemy carve him up like fresh sushi, or twist clear of these ropes and hurtle to the river below.

Choice One was *certain* death, Choice Two, just *very likely* death!

With a grunt, Moonshadow threw himself to one side. The descending *shinobi* sword narrowly missed his head, its twin blood grooves making a sound like tearing paper as it streaked through the air. As he evaded, one of the ropes across his back *twanged* around his elbow and Moonshadow fell backward, quickly turning upside down. Angry white water and the narrowing jaws of the gorge flashed below. As he plunged from the bridge, he glimpsed The Deathless dart to the edge and lean over, pulling something from his belt.

In a second, a tumult of last thoughts crackled through his mind...

He had failed, failed his order—his family—and the shogun himself.

Now he would die disgraced and the war he was supposed to prevent would devastate his country.

He had failed to save Snowhawk too, for any moment, with him dead, The Deathless would surely—

ACCORDING
TO LEGEND

Moonshadow cried out as his plunge was arrested with a harsh jolt and burning pain in one of his ankles. With his sword and free hand wheeling, he raised his head to glare up at the underside of the bridge. With an ankle-searing, eye-watering jerk, then another, he began to rise toward it. What was happening? Pain and heat bit his flesh again and as he focused on the source, his situation became clear.

A thin chain was wound around his ankle, a trembling chain that led straight to the hands of The Deathless. Moonshadow gaped. What speed this enemy had! Even as he had fallen, the assassin had snared his ankle with a small version of those capture chains that he and Snowhawk had barely evaded in Fushimi.

The Deathless leaned back hard, dragging the chain through one hand, reeling it in with the other. Moonshadow turned and dangled, rising one jarring stretch of links at a time, suspended like a captured beast. He set his teeth. What had made his foe bother to lasso him? He'd been about to die. Why hadn't The Deathless simply let him fall?

With a low grunt the killer hauled him up onto the bridge, swinging him by his ankles and dropping him hard so he struck the boards, back first, with a loud *whump*. Before the shock of the harsh landing had passed, The Deathless swung the tip of his sword with blinding speed to halt sharply at the side of Moonshadow's neck. Moonshadow froze.

"If you feel the need to bathe, runt, that's fine by me. But I can hardly let you go without first handing over those plans." The Deathless pressed the sword tip harder and Moonshadow felt it start to cut the outer layers of his skin. The assassin gave a cruel snigger. "Now: You do have those plans around your neck, don't you? Or did I spare you for nothing? Is *she* wearing them, perhaps?"

For only an instant the assassin's eyes flicked in Snowhawk's direction, but that was all the time Moonshadow needed. Without warning he drove his sword up, striking The Deathless's weapon away from his neck with a cold *shing!* Just as quickly Moonshadow curled forward to scramble between his attacker's legs.

The Deathless struck down impulsively, and his blade narrowly passed between Moonshadow's disappearing ankles to *thunk* into a bridge board, its tip sticking in the wood. Moonshadow turned, scooping up a length of the pooled chain, then, as The Deathless lifted one foot to stamp at him, he quickly looped the chain around his opponent's raised ankle.

Leading with his shoulder, Moonshadow pitched himself forward and rammed his enemy's other leg, forcing The Deathless off-balance. Stumbling, with his sword stuck in one of the bridge's boards and leg tangled in his own capture chain, The Deathless was forced to break off his attack.

Rolling out of his enemy's reach, Moonshadow snatched at his own end of the capture chain and hastily freed his ankle.

He leapt to his feet, raising his sword, as The Deathless hurriedly untangled the chain from his own leg. His eyes narrowed at Moonshadow, but not in rage. The Deathless grinned wickedly.

"That was amusing, runt! Nice to see you have at least *some* moves! But let's not get distracted from our real purpose, shall we?" He gave a knowing laugh. "It's you, isn't it? You're the one wearing the plans. I just spotted that small bulge on your chest!" Moonshadow tensed his jaw and scowled but made no answer. The Deathless sprinted forward, his speed and agility surprising Moonshadow. The gap between them closed in an instant, and as he charged, The Deathless snatched his sword free of the board. The bridge shook and swayed at the force of the killer's attack. His weapon turned horizontally in one hand and sliced for Moonshadow's neck.

Moonshadow barely ducked the powerful cut. His foe's blade hissed overhead and as its tip reached the end of its arc, Moonshadow bounced to his feet and hacked at The Deathless's arm. He felt his blade meet its target. Moonshadow gasped, amazed that he had actually been able to strike his legendary foe.

The tall assassin grunted and bolted back a few paces, jolting the bridge hard. A big cut appeared in his sleeve and skin showed through the gaping cloth, but there was no sign of blood, nor even of a wound.

Moonshadow's elation turned to horror and he flinched hard. So it was all true! *Immune to blades!*

He glanced back at the end of the bridge. Snowhawk had crept down to it. The cat had remounted the narrow walkway, about ten boards in, and was fearfully hunching low at every buck and swing of the bridge. Moonshadow waved at Snowhawk to run. She shook her head. He turned back toward The Deathless, raising his sword. Moonshadow ground his teeth. If she wouldn't run, then she might just have to watch him die. He shuffled for his enemy, frowning with concentration. But not if he could help it!

The Deathless hunched forward intently, as if thinking, then abruptly sheathed his sword. His hands flashed down into his belt and instantly rose again to lash the air hard as they each launched a tiny weapon.

Snowhawk shouted a warning, but Moonshadow already knew that poison-tipped hand darts were streaking at him. He ducked as the first dart's small flights parted wisps of his hair. The second dart tore past just above his shoulder. As he turned his head it closely crossed before his eyes with a faint *hiss*, a blurred, angular cluster of woven feathers bound to a hollow-tipped iron needle.

Moonshadow glared at his opponent. The Deathless had sheathed his sword in the middle of a duel! What arrogance! Moonshadow stood tall and ran forward, trying to close the distance quickly while his foe's weapon was still in its sheath.

His thoughts raced as he charged. Of course he'll draw as I attack, but I'll still have the advantage, for he's on the defensive... but how many darts does he have left? What if he draws one before I—

Just as he thought it, The Deathless pulled a third dart from his belt and swung back his throwing arm at a speed hard to follow with the eye. Desperate to arrest his crazed charge, Moonshadow flung himself to the bridge boards and, sliding painfully over their weathered, uneven joints, he steadily ground to a halt.

The Deathless tracked him with his eyes, taking careful aim. Moonshadow flinched and raised his left forearm defensively over his face as The Deathless hurled a poisoned dart.

The dart *whumped* hard into Moonshadow's left wrist, its flights twisting on impact to pucker the cloth of his sleeve. Behind him on the swaying bridge, the temple cat let out an eerie wail.

Moonshadow's face twisted. He gave a sharp moan, then collapsed.

UNDER A DARK SCIENCE

N o! No!" Snowhawk shrieked across the bridge. "Lord Hachiman's longest curses upon you, one called The Deathless! Stand your ground! I'm coming now to kill you myself!"

The assassin strode for Moonshadow. "Fine! Come then, die like your friend!" The Deathless called back indifferently. "Right after I collect my plans!" He dropped to one knee, looming over Moonshadow, hands spreading like talons around the bulge in his jacket where the bamboo tube held the doomsday musket plans. "And here they are!"

Moonshadow's knee suddenly rose and his foot

flashed up from the boards. The Deathless turned his head as Moonshadow's snapping kick connected with the side of it, knocking him away. Catching his balance, The Deathless reached for his sword, but Moonshadow leapt to his feet, took a long stride, then vaulted into a flying side kick.

The bridge lurched, making the cat meow again. Struck hard in the chest, The Deathless staggered backward, arms reeling.

Changing sword-hands, Moonshadow pulled back his punctured sleeve and tugged the poison dart from the armored forearm guard Akira had given him after their duel. Raising one eyebrow, he held the small missile up so The Deathless could see its ruined, flattened tip.

The Deathless blinked at the hidden armor and the foiled dart, as if astonished. Seizing on his apparent distraction, Moonshadow tossed the dart aside, gripped his sword with two hands, and dashed at his enemy, extended sword-tip leading the attack. The bridge rocked again.

If he could only get there in time, before—

The Deathless bent his knees, then launched himself into a powerful jump as Moonshadow closed with him. Startled by the move, Moonshadow broke his charge and bucked back. An instinct told him to *look up*. He did, in time to see The Deathless descending on him. Moonshadow flew into a turn, then dived forward into a roll, tumbling back along the bridge the way he had come.

The bridge boards pitched as The Deathless landed squarely with a loud *thump*. Moonshadow scrambled to his feet, turning back to face his foe, sword raised and ready. He panted, exchanging scowls with his nemesis and smelling his own frightened sweat. The Deathless drew his sword with lightning speed, ran, and pounced. He volleyed at Moonshadow, parrying his sword as he landed almost on top of him. Moonshadow was thrown off balance by the speed and closeness of the attack. Before he could recover into a defensive stance, The Deathless turned his sword like a striking snake and hacked at a sharp angle. Moonshadow growled with pain as his foe's blade dug into his shoulder. He struck it out and away with his own sword as a searing wave of heat spread outward from the cut. The Deathless lunged and, locking swords with Moonshadow, started pushing his lighter opponent down and backward. The bridge swung hard. The temple cat let out a terrified hiss.

"Poor runt! Is this the best you can do? *Moonshadow*, huh? Then let's see you shove me off, turn, and strike!" The big killer gave a heartless laugh. "Come, show me your fastest move, the way you showed poor Akira. Or are you tired now?" Forcing Moonshadow's sword down, The Deathless leaned over it sharply and head-butted his victim. There was a deep *thunk*. At the end of the bridge, Snowhawk gave a strangled scream.

Moonshadow sank to his knees, badly stunned, The Deathless towering over him. Their swords were still locked together, but Moonshadow was quickly losing strength and with it, he knew, the fight. But despite the awful blow to his head, his mind still worked with unexpected clarity. Think fast, he ordered himself, reason it out, as Mantis would say. Every fighter has a weakness, and even here, *there is a way*.

Most of his body had been conditioned to withstand tremendous impacts, but just one head-butt had swept him to the edge of mild concussion.

How? There was only one explanation: that had been no ordinary head-to-head impact. So The Deathless wore an armored forehead band under his bindings. Groggy as he felt, Moonshadow realized what that gave away. If The Deathless secretly wore *any* armor, then there existed some weapon or cut that he feared. So he *could* be cut. And what could be cut might also be scratched.

Moonshadow turned his aching head quickly. The cat was still there. He forced himself to split his failing energy two ways: half to sustain the sword clench, the rest to link with the cat as fast—and as completely—as possible.

So The Deathless liked to brag about levels of knowledge? This, Moonshadow thought with angry determination, was the eye of the beast, level three: sight-control.

"Enjoy it!" Moonshadow snarled up at his looming foe.

"Enjoy what?" The Deathless frowned.

Movement behind Moonshadow forced the killer to look up. Just as he did, a black-and-white ball of fur and fury landed on his upper chest. Locking its hind claws into his jacket, the temple cat attacked, fore-claws slashing again and again at the face of The Deathless. In between the frenzied strokes it hissed, spat, and tried to bite him.

Moonshadow saw his opponent reel backward. Breaking the sword clench, The Deathless nearly dropped his blade as he tried to pry the cat off. Such an attack presented any swordsman with quite a dilemma. Using his razor-edged blade on a thrashing, wriggling target stuck to his own body was just too risky. Vainly The Deathless struggled, briefly pulling the cat free only for it to spring back, renewing its assault.

His vision muted now by both the head-butt and the sight joining process, Moonshadow haphazardly gripped his sword and swung it at The Deathless's closest leg. As it struck home he realized that he had mistakenly attacked with the blunt edge leading. He was startled then when a dark, wet line appeared on his foe's leg, exactly where his edge had clubbed.

That was it! The secret of the dark science The Deathless lived under. Moonshadow set his jaw and struggled to his feet. The Deathless was immune to cutting edges. They were as blunt edges to him. *And the reverse was also true.*

Moonshadow raised his weapon. The Deathless was protecting his eyes with his sword hand, snatching blindly for the scruff of the cat's neck with his other. Moonshadow swung his sword, blunt side leading, low at The Deathless's belly. Again it felt as if he had merely clubbed his opponent. Then a line of blood appeared where Moonshadow's dull edge had struck.

The Deathless threw his head back, roaring with pain and anger. And something else perhaps, just a trace, of what Moonshadow never thought to hear in his voice. *Fear.*

His mind churned, trying to hatch a follow-up plan. Now that he knew how, he could wound The Deathless enough to make a run for it. But the killer still blocked the narrow bridge. How to get past him without risking another cut? And what about Snowhawk? Moonshadow's strength was ebbing fast, his wound and the demands of sight-control draining the *ki* from him by the second. But he rallied himself, aiming wild strikes at his enemy's legs.

Cutting the air with frenzied strokes, The Deathless fell backward onto the bridge. It twisted and swung, making Moonshadow snatch a grip on the nearest rope.

"I'm right behind you!" he heard Snowhawk snap. "Jump him, jump him *now!*"

The Deathless lay struggling, still trying to fling the cat off. Moonshadow hurdled over him, shaking the bridge, and the killer sensed his position. The double-grooved sword flashed up, cutting Moonshadow's thigh as he sailed overhead.

Moonshadow's wounded leg buckled as he landed. Stumbling, he fell to the bridge.

Snowhawk landed behind him unharmed. Now they were both on the rendezvous side of the bridge, with The Deathless and the cat, still locked in battle, in the center of it. The formerly invincible killer now thrashed about as if gripped with panic, sustaining new cuts from the blunt edge of his own sword. Obviously unaccustomed to the wounds most *shinobi* were trained to bear, perhaps to pain of any kind, he swatted at the cat with weakened, flailing strokes.

Together Snowhawk and Moonshadow looked back, and he handed her his sword.

"I'm calling the cat off now," Moonshadow said through gritted teeth. His eyes watered with pain and as he blinked, tears were forced down his cheeks.

Strands from a fraying support rope dangled to the foot planks of the bridge. Moonshadow began winding the thickest one around his wrist. "Do the same, then cut the bridge's main ropes," he told Snowhawk. His eyelids fluttered. "Then hang on! It should come apart."

Moonshadow's head sagged. Snowhawk cut the first of the four main ropes. The bridge lurched violently.

"Get out of there now!" she called to the cat. "Come on, playtime's over!" The cat ignored her, sustaining its crazed attack on The Deathless. Snow-hawk cut the second of the main ropes. The bridge lurched again, then pitched to a scarier angle.

Hanging on desperately, Moonshadow looked up, willing the cat to break off its assault. It finally

295

jumped from The Deathless and started bounding to Moonshadow, but behind it, The Deathless scrambled to his feet. Cursing, he swung wildly at where he *thought* the cat was. His fiery stroke narrowly missed the animal but cut the third main bridge rope.

"Hold on, Moonshadow, hold on!" Snowhawk yelled, snatching a wrist-tie for herself. The bridge twisted sideways and shuddered. It hung briefly by the fourth and final load-bearing rope while the thinner overhead supports snapped free noisily one by one. Then, with a nerve-wrenching *sssnap!* the last main rope broke and the bridge came apart near the middle, each end of its ragged halves trailing straggly ropes as they dropped.

The two falling sections of the bridge swung outward from the breaking point, pendulum-like, heading for the gorge walls their ends were still anchored to.

Starting to drop, The Deathless released his sword and snatched for the nearest escaping strand of rope. But the force of the swinging bridge whipped it away from his hands and he plunged.

As their half of the bridge swung toward the rock wall, Moonshadow glanced down into the gorge. He caught a last glimpse of The Deathless. The assassin tumbled, head over heels, toward the white water below. Yet as he fell, his arms and legs weren't flailing, as if somehow, at the last, he'd regained his icy calm.

Moonshadow's eyes flicked around the gorge, but he saw no sign of the cat.

He looked up. Impact with the rock wall was perhaps two seconds away.

Gritting his teeth, he closed his eyes tightly.

BEYOND THE IMPACT

The severed section of bridge slapped against the gorge's rocky side, and Moonshadow and Snowhawk cried out as they were jolted hard. The ropes wound about their wrists tightened sharply and burned their skin.

For half a minute they dangled, summoning up their last reserves of strength for the climb to safety. Then painfully, each fighting exhaustion as well as injuries, they unwound the wrist-ropes and clawed their way up, using the bridge's remaining planks and lines as a ladder. Snowhawk reached the lip of the gorge first and held a trembling hand out for

Moonshadow's. He gripped her wrist. She pulled him up.

Leaning on each other, the pair staggered uphill to the edge of the next forest.

"We rest here." Snowhawk propped Moonshadow against a log. She took a scarf from inside her jacket and tied a field dressing on his shoulder wound. "Is there a backup meeting place, in case—" She looked over her shoulder. "Wait. My head is clear now and I *know* I sense *shinobi* energy."

A bush rustled about ten paces behind her. Moonshadow turned his head wearily. He and Snowhawk were in pretty bad shape. If it *wasn't* his people, could they defeat even some old cleaning lady now? He wasn't sure.

Groundspider rose from the center of the bush. He wore a tree-and-leaf patterned camouflage suit with the hood pulled back, a large backpack, and a sword slung from one shoulder. He frowned and pointed at Moonshadow.

"So it *is* you!" Groundspider broke into a grin.

"The girl here had me confused. What's the story with her? A hostage?"

Moonshadow and Snowhawk exchanged tired, relieved smiles.

"Not a hostage," Moonshadow told Groundspider,

299

"a new ally, with valuable knowledge. She comes back with us, or I don't come back."

"Really?" Groundspider's eyebrows arched. "Haven't *we* grown bold on our first outing? An ally, huh? Well then I assume *one of you* has the plans?"

They both nodded. Moonshadow patted the bamboo tube inside his jacket.

After heaving a relieved sigh, Groundspider bowed to Snowhawk. Then he turned to Moonshadow and shook his big head with envy and astonishment. "And to think I was wondering how you would cope, out here in the big, bad world!"

Moonshadow glanced at him sideways. "Let's talk about it later. Were you *late*?"

"Yeah, but not my fault. I was caught up in an incident on the highway while traveling in disguise. Some idiot ronin tried to make me hire him as a bodyguard. Hah! Do *I* look like I need protection? Well, he wouldn't take *no* for an answer and it led to swords."

"Some people never learn." Moonshadow smiled knowingly. Snowhawk gave him a questioning look. "Tell you another time…" he whispered.

"But that was not the worst of it!" Groundspider cracked his knuckles. "Just because I cut this fool's ear off, a passing inspector made me file a report. For a while there, I thought I'd have to fight *him* too! Convinced him it was self-defense, and my skillful cut a bit of mere luck on my part. But I still had to pay a price. Paperwork! It took hours. And the forms, you should have seen the forms! Whoever makes those things up must be a madman—"

"You *must* be Groundspider." Snowhawk laughed. He blinked at her with surprise.

"Filling out forms? You have truly suffered." Moonshadow sighed. "Any idea what's keeping the others?"

"They shot me a coded message arrow three hills back. They were delayed by roadblocks manned by a scruffy bunch of drunken gangsters. But they're only about ten minutes away now." Groundspider glanced at Snowhawk then gave Moonshadow a strange, respectful smirk. "Wait till they hear about *this*!"

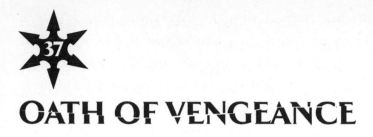

OATH OF VENGEANCE

Silver Wolf scowled bitterly, then motioned to the samurai guard to send his visitor in.

"Then close the doors, keep all others away," he ordered, examining his empty sake cup. His head ached from drinking too much the night before. At least it had helped him forget things for an hour or two. His empty audience chamber was eerily silent, yet another reminder of his terrible defeat. Silver Wolf hung his head and paced to the small padded platform. He sat down, dropping the cup onto the dais beside him.

Private Investigator Katsu entered the chamber and bowed to his master.

Silver Wolf motioned for him to sit. "Have you spent the bribe money I gave you?" The warlord folded his arms into his silken sleeves.

Katsu nodded. "It was required, Lord. Yes, sadly, it is all gone."

"Then, for your sake, Detective, I hope it produced results. Someone's going to pay for this... failed operation. It's been expensive in every way. Plans gone. Akira and Jiro each left useless, at least for the foreseeable future. My top swordsman badly hurt. His sidekick too. Both out of action for months. Most incredible of all, I'm told that The Deathless himself is missing, presumed slain! Now, who exactly has done all this to me? You had better know, Detective."

"I've tried to make sense of scraps of information from useful, though expensive, informants, and also to draw conclusions from certain things witnesses— an old local watchman for example—were able to tell me. It's my unhappy duty to confirm your worst suspicions, Lord." Katsu gave an extra little bow. "I believe the nuisance who did this indeed hails from the Grey Light Order. It seems, in the end, he either somehow recruited the support of that female spy your men trailed, or possibly took her prisoner after Jiro had wounded her. Some of the accounts are conflicting, some a little confused. But the boy, the one who cut Akira quite badly, appears to be from the Grey Light Order. These dogs of the shogun train in a monastery in Edo. As my Lord may have heard, they are an independent force, with, it is said, members from both Iga and Koga shadow clan training backgrounds. Like many spy groups, they accept suitable orphans for training as agents."

"Very well!" Silver Wolf closed his fist. "So he is a Grey Light creation!" He took a deep breath, barely hanging on to his self-control. "Now the greatest question of all. What is the name of my *number one target* from this day on?"

Katsu gave a triumphant smile. "The nuisance is called Moonshadow, Lord."

"Moonshadow?" Silver Wolf raised one eyebrow. "Like the sword move?"

"Yes, Lord. Apparently such namings are a custom among the *shinobi*." Katsu took a folded page of notes from his jacket. Silver Wolf rolled his eyes as Katsu studied it at length. "Ah, yes, here's another example, Lord: one of my informers mentioned a spy whose name was Great Downward Rushing Wind, also the name of a complex sword move."

"Yes, yes! Fascinating!" The warlord wagged a finger irritably. "But tell me *this*! Why was the little insect, a mere orphan boy after all, so effective?"

"I learned that, young as he is, he employs the eye of the beast, that Old Country skill, thought—until recently—to have died out forever. He can influence animals, my Lord, bend them to his will, use them as *his* spies. Or so the lost art was described to me."

"Mmmm." Silver Wolf gave a resigned sigh. "Good job...as usual." He dipped in his lavish jacket and threw Katsu a small purse. "That's the balance of your fees, plus the standard advance on your next assignment. I need you to return to your native Edo. Learn all you can about the Grey Light Order." His voice thickened with hatred. "They want a shadow war? They will get it! I'll crush them. I *swear* I will. Now, one final, tactical question. Who hates them more than anyone else? Even more than I do at this moment!"

The detective consulted his interview notes. "Their arch enemies are the oldest shadow clan, Lord. The House of Fuma."

Silver Wolf stood up and stared at the window,

turning his back on the investigator. "I'll be writing a sealed letter to them, seeking an alliance. Come back and collect it tomorrow before you set off. On your way to Edo, there's a certain teahouse on the highway where you need leave it." He waved a dismissal. "That is all!"

Katsu stood and bowed low before leaving. "As always, it's an honor to serve you."

As the doors closed behind his visitor, Silver Wolf snatched up his sake cup and hurled it at the window. The cup hit the sill and shattered into tiny pieces.

"*Moonshadow*?" he snarled. "I'll break him like *that*! I will have his *head*!"

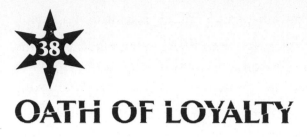

OATH OF LOYALTY

Gently rubbing his shoulder bandage, Moonshadow limped through the sunlit garden of the Edo safe house. It was hidden at the end of a quiet, leafy street, far from the fortress-like walls of the Grey Light Order's monastery.

Snowhawk sat on a flat stone bench that offered an ideal view of the large carp pond. Moonshadow smiled as he watched her stare dreamily at the water. Maple and cherry trees ringed the deep pond. Gold and red fish bobbed to the surface, quietly hunting insects. It was a scene of peace and harmony. It was the opposite of how they lived.

She glanced up and smiled. He sat down beside her. They looked at each other and exchanged nods.

"Congratulations," he said, looking away quickly, "I just heard the good news. They have accepted your oath of loyalty. So, having given it, you can stay."

"I still have a final test to pass, involving an interview with someone called the White Nun. But whatever happens, to have come even this far... I owe it all to your support." She bowed. "It's the reason they've given me this chance."

"No," he said firmly. "They've taken you in because of your great skills."

"It was hard, you know, a few days back." Snowhawk hung her head. "As part of proving my new allegiance to the Grey Light Order, I had to divulge everything about the clan who reared me, my former clients, my missions. All of it! To speak of such things goes against a spy's nature, but I made myself tell them what they wanted to know." She smiled gratefully at him. "As you did for me, back in that chalk cave."

"Mantis said it was Clan Fuma who sent you to Fushimi for the plans... for *themselves*, not for a client."

"Yes. They intended to auction the plans to the highest bidder among the rebel warlords. Silver Wolf is not the only malcontent. The shogun has many enemies. Your order seems to truly believe in this new age of peace, that enough blood has been spilled during the long civil war years. This might sound strange, but I hope you're all willing to fight hard for that peace, for many lords would gladly murder it." Snowhawk shrugged. "So now it seems that I too must fight for peace, not for glory, revenge, or profit as I was reared to...in a hard school." She looked at him with sadness in her eyes. "I will try, I will try to live in the way of your order, to think in its way too." A shadow crossed her face. "That may not come easily to me. Fuma train suitable orphans, just as Grey Light do. But hear my words, they are nowhere near as kind to them. By many means, they put fire in our veins, ice into our hearts. Now I am—supposedly—free of their stain, but can a bird just change the way it flies?"

"That's all behind you now," Moonshadow said. "They do things properly here. Brother Eagle will have you schooled in certain methods only *we* use, then he'll assign you to somebody. You'll work with them for a few missions, kind of as an apprentice."

She frowned suspiciously. "Any idea who they might put me with?"

Moonshadow shrugged and tried to sound casual. "Somebody around your age, but still really good..."

Snowhawk rolled her eyes. "Really good and, I guess, really humble..."

"Hey, none of that!" He glanced at her sideways. "After all, who flipped you off the rain roof?"

"Who, just before that, could have easily killed you on that rain roof?"

He scowled at her. "Who got you out of Fushimi despite three expert enemies?"

"Who put you to sleep in Fushimi with three little glances?" She folded her arms.

"Yeah, well I'd like to see you try *that* again," Moonshadow mumbled.

"Sure," Snowhawk whispered, "just look this way, tough guy."

Moonshadow hesitated, then held his nose in the air. "I don't *feel* like doing that right now!"

A sound made the pair look around. Heron entered the garden carrying a basket covered with a rug. Snowhawk and Moonshadow stood up and bowed to her.

Heron flashed her gentle, stately smile and patted the basket. A weak *meow* came from under the leaf-patterned rug. "Your report mentioned a certain friendly temple cat. An ideal sight-joining subject, you wrote, with a tail its kind don't usually possess."

She uncovered the basket and the cat sat up, meowing excitedly.

"Imagine our surprise," Heron went on, "when a sopping wet animal of just that description turned up at our Tokaido safe inn near Fushimi. I'm told the poor creature was badly bruised and appeared to be half drowned."

"Were you looking for me?" Moonshadow asked the cat. He gently took it from the basket and held it against his chest. It immediately started purring. "I don't even know if it's a boy or a girl, but I owe this cat my life." He looked to Snowhawk.

Snowhawk nodded. "We both owe it a debt, for the destruction of The Deathless."

Moonshadow frowned at her words. Could anyone be sure The Deathless *had* been slain? He stared down at the temple cat. After all, *it* had somehow survived the river.

"It seems *she* wants to be your mascot." Heron's fingers glided along the cat's spine. The animal arched its back against her touch and its tail gave a satisfied flick. "Or perhaps, simply another new friend." She smiled warmly at Snowhawk. "Our Moonshadow seems to have a talent for bringing home great prizes and making new friends...in your case, one might say, both at once."

Snowhawk beamed at Heron. "You are too kind."

Moonshadow stroked the cat's neck and its purring grew louder. Suddenly he put it back into Heron's basket and folded his arms.

Heron studied him and then spoke softly. "Moonshadow-Kun. How I know that look and stance! It means something weighs heavily on your mind." She put down the basket.

Moonshadow slowly shrugged. "Before I went on this mission, my first real mission, I often thought of myself as one who'd forever be alone. Fate has been kind. It has shown me that I'm not." He glanced from Heron to Snowhawk and back. "I have both family and friends. And you know what? It doesn't matter if one's family or friends are unusual, few, or as unique as this cat. Those who truly care for you are the great stones of your castle's wall."

"Ever true, and well said." Heron sounded proud of him. "So why the storm clouds in your eyes?"

"Because now I also have an enemy." Moonshadow glanced at Snowhawk. "A man with ambition, wealth, and power. A man who won't forget either of us."

Heron patted his shoulders. "A man you will never face alone."

✦ Glossary ✦

Amida (as in Lord Amida): Pronounced *ah-me-dah*. Buddhist spiritual being revered by many in feudal Japan. Amida is known as Amita−bha in other parts of Asia.

Ashiko: Pronounced *ah-she-koh*. Detachable foot spikes, usually used along with **shuko** (pronounced *shoo-koh*) or climbing claws, they helped spies climb trees, cross ice, scale walls, and even defend themselves.

Bo: Pronounced *boh*. A hard wooden quarterstaff used in both Japan and Okinawa for close combat.

Bokken: Pronounced *boh-ken*. A Japanese training weapon, carved from heavy wood in the shape of a samurai sword. Some bokken even come with a matching carved (or in modern times plastic) scabbard.

Ezo: Pronounced *eh-zoh*. One of many former names for Hokkaido, the second largest and northernmost of Japan's main islands.

Furube sutra Pronounced *foo-roo-beh*. Literally "The Shrugging Off" or "Shaking Off." An ancient saying or prayer of preparation, recited by *shinobi* each dawn and dusk, and just before going into action. It was intended to clear the spy's mind of distractions, calm them, and ready their skills. The *furube* sutra's parts could be described as the Preparation Verse, the Facing Self Verse, and the Verse of One Resolved. Each "verse" translates as a single line in English. The text of the sutra can be interpreted in a number of ways when translated from Japanese. Below is one possible rendering, kindly translated by Iaido expert and scholar Dr. Yasuhisa Watanabe and reworded by the author for tonal and dramatic purposes. See also **Sutra**.

Gather, tidy, and align your ways, for they bring karma. Cleanse any lies made this day, scatter not one grain of life. To end this path in happiness, seek peace within your mind.

Go: *Five* in Japanese. Pronounced as it reads, it can also be a name, part of a name, or a nickname.

Hachiman (as in Lord Hachiman): Pronounced *hah-chee-maan*. Shinto god of war, divine protector of Japan and its people, whose symbolic animal and messenger, perhaps ironically from a western viewpoint, is a dove, the Biblical symbol of peace. According to legend, Emperor Ojin, a mortal, became the divine Hachiman. After Buddhism's arrival in Japan, Hachiman was also associated with the Buddhist deity Daibosatsu. Both peasants and samurai worshipped Hachiman in medieval times, and to this day there remain over 30,000 shrines to the war god throughout Japan.

Iaido: Pronounced *ee-eye-doh*. The samurai art of sword-drawing and dueling, which features about fifty different *waza* (techniques) and reached the peak of its development around five hundred years ago. Different from Kendo, which is a full-contact sport.

Modern students of Iaido use steel swords in wooden scabbards and wear the traditional clothing of medieval samurai. Iaido takes many years to master. To this day, the art's world titles are held in Japan, on a mountaintop near Kyoto, before a Japanese prince. Author Simon Higgins has competed in this event as well as in Australia's national Iaido titles. See also **Tsukikage**.

Kami: Pronounced *car-mee*. The Japanese term for objects of awe or worship in Shintoism, Japan's oldest (and native) religion. Though sometimes translated as "deity" or "gods," this is not strictly accurate and "spirits" may be a safer way of describing the Kami, who can be "beings" but also simply forces of nature or "living essences."

Kan: Pronounced *can*. A traditional Japanese unit for measuring mass. One kan equals about 3.75 kilograms.

Karma: Pronounced *car-ma*. The Buddhist philosophy that states that deeds or actions create cycles of cause and effect. Thus, good thinking and good deeds produce good outcomes, now or at some time in the future. Brother Mantis, Moonshadow's dueling coach, is particularly wary of actions that may bring bad karma.

Ki: Pronounced *kee*. The life force common to all living things. Internal or spiritual energy, which in traditional Asian martial arts is harnessed to increase a warrior's power and stamina. Using ancient sciences like sight joining can quickly deplete a *shinobi*'s *ki*.

Kimono: Pronounced *kee-mo-no*. Literally means "something worn." T-shaped, ankle-length robes worn by men, women, and children of all classes. Recognizably the traditional clothing of the Japanese.

Kirishima: Pronounced *ki-ri-shee-mah*. The Japanese name by which the country's colorful native azaleas were first known. It derives from the flowering plant's home locality: Kirishima is a mountain in Kagoshima Prefecture in Southern Kyushu.

Koga: Pronounced *koh-gah*. Like Iga (pronounced *ee-gah*), a name associated with a mountain region of Japan in which "shadow clans" trained highly skilled contract spies and assassins whose powers of stealth and disguise became legendary. Author Simon Higgins visited a preserved three-hundred-year-old Koga ninja house that features a display of weapons and tools and, beneath a trap door, an underground escape passage. It stands near Konan railway station in farming country outside Kyoto.

-Kun: When pronounced, the *u* takes on an *oo* sound. An honorific used by seniors when addressing their juniors. It is generally reserved for males, but sometimes used when referring to a *young* female. Also used as a term of affection. See also **-San**.

Mochi: Pronounced *mo-chee*. Traditional Japanese sweets. Attractively wrapped in special paper, *mochi* vary in size, color and style throughout Japan. They may contain unusual textures and flavors derived from plums, chestnuts, or various vegetables. Author Simon Higgins became addicted to *mochi* on his first trip to Japan in 1982.

Moonshadow: See **Tsukikage.**

Naginata: Pronounced *na-gi-na-ta.* A weapon consisting of a long pole fitted with a curved, single-edged blade. Sometimes used by spies, the short *naginata* was also a favorite weapon of high-born samurai women, being ideally suited for self-defense indoors.

Ronin: Pronounced *roh-nin.* Literally "wave men"— unemployed samurai, warriors who had lost their ruling lord through military defeat, death, or some other disbandment of his fiefdom. Many roamed the country, dueling or taking work as bodyguards, mercenaries, or assassins.

Sake: Pronounced *sah-kay.* Japanese for "alcoholic beverage," it can refer to alcoholic drinks in general, but usually refers to the traditional Japanese drink made by fermenting polished rice. Though often called "rice wine," sake is actually brewed, so is really more like beer than wine.

Samurai: Pronounced *sa-moo-rye*. A member of the ruling warrior class; a warrior in a warlord's service.

-San: The *a* is pronounced with a slight *u* sound as in *sun*. An honorific attached to a person's name to show one is addressing them with respect. It can be taken to mean "Mr.," "Mrs.," "Miss," or, nowadays, "Ms."

Shinobi: Pronounced *shi-no-bee*. Also known as *ninja*, pronounced *nin-jah*. Those adept at spying or covert scouting. Some *shinobi* were also hired killers. They were trained in a wide variety of secret and martial arts, said to include combat with and without weapons, acrobatics, the use of explosives, poisons, traps, hypnotism, and numerous forms of disguise. Some of the most effective historical *ninja* were women who went "undercover" inside well-guarded fortresses, successfully stealing information or carrying out assassinations.

Shogun: Pronounced s*how-gun*. Abbreviated form of *Sei-I-Tai Shogun* ("barbarian subduing general"). The ultimate commander of the Japanese warrior class who, prior to 1867, exercised virtually absolute rule (officially) under the leadership of the emperor, who was in fact a figurehead only. Most warlords aspired to seize or earn this auspicious rank.

Shuko: Pronounced *shoo-koh*. Iron claws worn on the hands to assist climbing. *Shuko* were used, usually along with **ashiko** (foot spikes) to scale walls and climb up trees, cross icy surfaces, and even during combat.

Shuriken: Pronounced *shoo-ri-ken*. Circular or star-shaped throwing knives, usually black and made in ingots or from thin sheets of iron. They could have four, eight, twelve, or more points. Each "shadow clan" or spy group used their own distinctive style or styles of *shuriken*. Thrown overarm, they were aimed for soft points such as the throat, eyes, or temple. Their tips could be poisoned or flecked with a powerful sedative if the target was to be taken alive. Any *shuriken* wound disrupted and weakened an enemy.

Sutra: Pronounced *soo-tra*. A "scripture" of the Buddhist faith; teachings that were sometimes chanted or recited to focus and empower the devotee. See also **Furube sutra**.

Temple cat (also called **Kimono cat**): A patterned cat, respected in Japan for centuries, whose back markings are said to resemble a woman in a kimono, hence their other name. Considered sacred, these cats usually have a stumpy, triangular tail. They are still found in many parts of Japan. Author Simon Higgins has photographed Kimono cats in the temples of central Tokyo (known in Moonshadow's time as Edo).

Tengu: Pronounced *teng-goo*. According to the superstitions of Old Japan, a long-nosed, tree-dwelling mountain devil, fond of lurking in the canopies of cryptomeria (Japanese cedar) trees. *Tengu* were often blamed for missing travelers, who were more likely the victims of bandits.

Tetsubishi: Pronounced *tet-soo-bi-she*. Also known as *makibishi* or (in Europe) caltrops. Sharp, usually triple-spiked foot jacks made from seed pods, iron, or twisted wire. The jack's tips were sometimes flecked with poison. They could be painted to blend in with reed matting or a polished wooden floor. Able to penetrate sandals, *tetsubishi* caused unexpected injuries, stopping or slowing a pursuer.

Torii (gate): Pronounced *toh-ree*. A simple, usually three- or four-beamed, wooden archway found at the entrance to a Shinto shrine. Often painted red, a *torii* gate signified entering a place visited by both spirits and the living. Throughout medieval times, Shinto, the native religion of Japan, and Buddhism, which had more recently spread to Japan from China, existed peacefully side by side.

Travel Guidebooks (in Old Japan): Even in medieval times, the Japanese, despite the many dangers their land frequently presented, were enthusiastic tourists, and an entire industry developed around publishing travel guidebooks, some of them illustrated. But as a reference in *Moonshadow* (concerning Snowhawk's thoughts) implies, the guidebooks were not always reliable, some containing sensational, convenient, or misleading information.

Tsukikage: Pronounced *skee-car-geh*. A 470-year-old sword *waza* (technique) of the Musou Jikiden Eishin-Ryu school of Iaido, the art of the samurai sword. The Moonshadow technique employs a low, delayed turn, then rising at the attacking foe and executing a crescent strike at their raised forearms. This combination block-and-cut is followed by a push, then a step, after which a fatal single vertical cut is unleashed. The characters making up the technique's name can be translated as "moonshadow." See also **Iaido**.

Water spiders (mizu gumo): Pronounced *mi-zoo-goo-mo*. Circular foot floats on which a spy balanced in order to cross a moat, pond, or still river. Only those of very light build could operate them. Festival sideshows in modern Japan still tempt contestants to take the *"mizu gumo* challenge" and try to cross a shallow "moat" with round floats on their feet. The rare successes (usually children) take home prizes. The rest get a free bath. Some historians believe that the *mizu gumo* design used by Koga *shinobi* was actually a single wooden lifebuoy or flotation ring, inside which the spy was suspended, submerged to the chest. Below the ring, small foot-mounted paddles helped propel him forward.

Yojimbo: Pronounced *yoh-jim-boh*. A bodyguard or security officer. Most *yojimbo* in historical Japan were either trusted samurai retainers assigned to guard their lord's life and family, or were hirelings, **ronin** (see above) whose need for income and evident sword skills made them a reliable choice of protector, say for a traveling merchant or performer forced to enter a war zone or a region plagued by bandits. In reality, many so-called *yojimbo* were really little more than hired assassins or, at the other end of the scale, the equivalent of modern western "bouncers" or security guards, keeping the peace outside a tavern or guarding a vulnerable warehouse.

Author's note and acknowledgments

The Moonshadow stories are fantasy tales set in a romanticized historical Japan. Though they reflect certain key events of the early Tokugawa era, and include many facts and details about the sword art of Iaido and Japanese warrior culture in general, they remain adventure yarns, not histories. Despite the many liberties I have taken, I hope these stories inspire readers of all ages to investigate the saga and customs of fascinating Old Japan, a world that still has so much to teach us.

My heartfelt thanks to the following real-life allies of the Grey Light Order: in the US, the wonderful *shinobi* of Clan Little, Brown, especially Alvina Ling, Connie Hsu, and Melanie Sanders, who truly have the Old Country skill of insight. In Australia and Japan, my lovely wife Annie, Catherine Drayton, the team at Random House Australia, Lian Hearn, Dr. Yasuhisa Watanabe, Nobutaka Tezuka, "Iron Chef" Hibiki Ito, and tea person, author and Tokonoma advocate Margaret Price. A very low bow to Dr. Glenn Stockwell, resident of Japan, Chief Instructor of Seishinkan Iaido Dojo, and a truly inspiring modern samurai.

To any readers wishing to learn more about the graceful art of Iaido, please visit:

www.seishinkan-iaido.org

✳ About the Author ✳

Simon Higgins's employment history reads like a novel. He's worked as a disc jockey, laboratory assistant, marketing manager, and even as a monster on a ghost train. He also spent a decade in law enforcement; as a police officer, state prosecutor and as a licensed private investigator.

Simon is proudly a student of Eishin-Ryu Iaido, a 470-year-old style of swordsmanship which prizes traditional techniques and medieval samurai etiquette and courtesy. He has trained in Japan and participated in Taikai (contests) before His Imperial Highness Prince Munenori Kaya, and, in 2008, he placed fifth in the Iaido World Titles held near Kyoto. In 2009, Simon was awarded a black belt by masters from the All Japan Iaido Federation.

www.simonhiggins.net